Everything yo
—a

WORLD'S MOST ELIGIBLE BACHELOR
Harrison Lawless

Occupation: "CEO. And a damn good one!"

Biggest Problem in Life: "Very pregnant women. I never realized how temperamental they were until I was stuck in close quarters with one. Now, how am I supposed to bulldoze this sweet, vulnerable woman like I do everyone else?"

Best Personality Trait: "I'm a take-charge kind of guy. It's the only way I can get things done the way I want. Some might call me arrogant, but I don't care. When it comes to landing a deal—or bedding a woman—I always get my way."

Dream Vacation: "A man in my position doesn't spend his days dreaming of vacations."

Marriage Vow: "Who said anything about marriage? I've got wealth, I've got power. That doesn't mean I need a bride—or a baby!"

Dear Reader,

The WORLD'S MOST ELIGIBLE BACHELORS continues with another brand-new story focusing on those irresistible creatures we know and love…men.

Every month we'll bring you the story of a to-die-for hero named by fictitious *Prominence Magazine* as one of the twelve World's Most Eligible Bachelors. As you turn the pages of these scintillating stories you'll get all the hot details about the romances that have these confirmed bachelors pulling out the engagement rings and falling to their knees.

This month, bestselling author Dixie Browning brings us an unforgettable bachelor—CEO Harrison Lawless. This powerful executive has been forced to trade in his three-piece suit for a pair of well-worn jeans, and learn to relax. But you won't be able to rest once you start reading how a pregnant and penniless woman tames the cantankerous businessman. This compelling story is also part of Dixie's series THE LAWLESS HEIRS.

And be sure to join us next month for a sexy hero that only innovative author Maggie Shayne could create for her series THE TEXAS BRAND. In *That Mysterious Texas Brand Man* you'll meet a hero cloaked in danger and desperately in need of a good woman's love.

Here's to romance wishes and bachelor kisses!

The Editors

Please address questions and book requests to:
Silhouette Reader Service
U.S.: 3010 Walden Ave., P.O. Box 1325, Buffalo, NY 14269
Canadian: P.O. Box 609, Fort Erie, Ont. L2A 5X3

World's Most
Eligible Bachelors

Dixie Browning

His Business, Her Baby

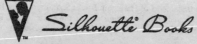

Silhouette Books

Published by Silhouette Books
America's Publisher of Contemporary Romance

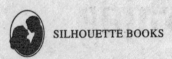 SILHOUETTE BOOKS

ISBN 0-373-65020-5

HIS BUSINESS, HER BABY

Copyright © 1998 by Dixie Browning

All rights reserved. Except for use in any review, the reproduction
or utilization of this work in whole or in part in any form by any
electronic, mechanical or other means, now known or hereafter
invented, including xerography, photocopying and recording, or in
any information storage or retrieval system, is forbidden without
the written permission of the editorial office, Silhouette Books,
300 East 42nd Street, New York, NY 10017 U.S.A.

All characters in this book have no existence outside the imagination of
the author and have no relation whatsoever to anyone bearing the same
name or names. They are not even distantly inspired by any individual
known or unknown to the author, and all incidents are pure invention.

This edition published by arrangement with Harlequin Books S.A.

® and TM are trademarks of Harlequin Books S.A., used under license.
Trademarks indicated with ® are registered in the United States Patent
and Trademark Office, the Canadian Trade Marks Office and in other
countries.

Printed in U.S.A.

A Conversation with...
RITA Award-winning author
DIXIE BROWNING

What hero have you created for WORLD'S MOST ELIGIBLE BACHELORS, and how has he earned the coveted title?

DB: Harrison Lancaster Lawless, founder, chief stockholder and, until recently, CEO of Lawless, Inc., has been called arrogant, controlling and coldhearted. The one thing he's never been called is stupid. But when it's all work and no play, something's got to give. In the case of *His Business, Her Baby*, what gives is Harrison. Reluctantly, but in all the best ways.

This original title is part of THE LAWLESS HEIRS, a Silhouette Desire miniseries. What about this series so appeals to you? Do you have spinoffs planned?

DB: THE LAWLESS HEIRS began with the question, what if? What if none of the heirs knew about the others? What if they meet someone special in the search for their heritage? So far I've met three Lawless cousins. Currently in the works, (and driving me wild, because if ever a guy was a rogue, this one is) is the story of yet another cousin. Watch for his debut in February 1999.

What modern-day personality best epitomizes a WORLD'S MOST ELIGIBLE BACHELOR?

DB: I wouldn't dare suggest any public personality. A man's public persona is usually a fabrication that bears little resemblance to his real character. After forty-eight years of marriage, I'd have to nominate my husband. He's not perfect—neither, to my amazement, am I—but he wears well.

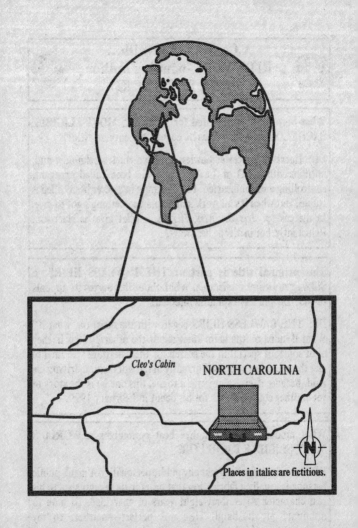

Cleo's Cabin

NORTH CAROLINA

Places in italics are fictitious.

One

Stress was a killer. Dump it or die. For weeks on end, those words had been ricocheting through his mind. Harrison Lancaster Lawless, founder, chief stockholder and, until recently, CEO of Lawless Inc., had been called a lot of things, including arrogant, stubborn and hard-nosed. He'd been called a bloody-minded, coldhearted pirate as well as a domineering control freak.

The one thing he had never been called was stupid. So, if he had to move out of the fast lane, after having led the pack for years, he would do it.

But he'd damned well do it his way.

And this, he thought, surveying the sprawling log house—three spacious wings, each with its own deck, surrounding a tall central portion, tucked away in a hidden cove on the shore of the Alligator River—was the way he intended to do it. In style, comfort and privacy. Once he was settled in he could have a few pieces of equipment shipped down, take his time set-ting them up, and before long, he'd have another company up and running.

Single-handed. In less than a year. Three years from now he'd have it on the stock exchange. Nothing like a challenge to get a man's juices flowing.

Right. Nothing like going flat out, twenty-two hours a day, year after year, maxing out your stress levels before you even down your fourth cup of morning coffee.

Swearing quietly, Harrison shoved his sunglasses to the top of his head. The trouble was, after thirty-seven years, he knew himself too well. Some kids inherited red hair. Some inherited flat feet. He'd inherited a competitive streak a mile wide. Cutting down was not an option. It was a case of cut loose completely, get out of range of temptation or end up back in the coronary care unit.

Or six feet under.

Okay, so he'd take the time to smell the damned roses.

Turning his back on the log house, he watched as two yachts, a yawl, a houseboat and another sailboat—part of the annual snowbird migration—headed north along the Intracoastal Waterway. He had friends who sailed. He'd always wondered how any man with a functioning brain could be content to do nothing but drift with the wind.

He had a feeling he was about to find out.

Swinging open the door of his dusty new Land Rover, he forced himself to watch until the last boat had passed. Forced himself to breathe deeply of the fresh, resinous air. Sooner or later he'd have to get used to it, but right now he'd give a big block of his own stock for the familiar stench of exhaust fumes, the blare of taxis and the hordes of humanity moving in restless eddies along city sidewalks. There was an energy in New York, in London, in Hong Kong. Here, there was nothing.

Correction. There had to be something. No place was completely devoid of energy. It was up to him to tune in to it, harness it and learn to use it appropriately if he was going to thrive. Or even survive.

And genetics or no genetics, he was damned well going to survive, if it killed him. A man who couldn't control his own stress levels didn't deserve to control a multibillion-dollar enterprise. Harrison had always prided himself on being in control of every aspect of his life, right up until the gods had decided to knock him off his throne.

So here he was. And here he damned well intended to stay. In the land, supposedly, of his roots. The land of peace and harmony.

The land of lethal boredom.

He'd almost missed the unmarked dirt road after miles of nothing but trees, swamp and farmland. Acting on sheer instinct, he'd veered off Highway 64 and followed it.

He might have missed the house completely, so well did it blend in with its surroundings. But two things had caught his attention. A blue-and-white For Sale sign and a yellow-print nightgown flapping on a clothesline. A *big* nightgown, more in the style of Pillsbury Mills than Victoria's Secret.

Eyes narrowed against the brilliant, late May sunshine, he studied the sprawling log house surrounded by weeds, the nondescript sedan parked out front, the lack of any attempt at landscaping. Mentally collecting, collating and filing away data, he reached the conclusion that, overgrown and undermaintained or not, it was just what the doctor ordered.

For one thing, it was far enough off the beaten track

that he wouldn't need to worry about nosy reporters. He'd given all the interviews he intended to give concerning the rise and fall of H. L. Lawless. What was that old song? "If they could see me now, dah-dah-dah-dadadah," he sang tunelessly. Boat watching from the front deck, bird watching from the back. God, how would he stand all the excitement?

And yet...for the first time in over a year, since his whole world had come crashing down around him, Harrison Lawless was conscious of a small undercurrent of optimism.

Cleo wandered out from the kitchen, a bowl of ice cream in one hand, a book of names in the other. For a full week now she'd been thinking about names instead of concentrating on what she'd come here to do. What had happened to the organized, capable, competent woman who had mailed out all those résumés and set forth to sell the lodge, find a new job, establish herself in a new home and get started on building a new life?

Lately she'd had trouble remembering her own name, yet here she was, trying to decide on a name for someone else. As for deciding what to do with the remains of her past, it was simply beyond her.

For three weeks, ever since she'd driven down from Chesapeake and signed all those papers in the real estate office, putting the lodge on the market, she'd been drifting along in a warm pink cloud of prepartum euphoria, unable to concentrate on anything.

What to take, what to leave behind? How could she decide that when she didn't even know where she'd be going? So far, she hadn't had a response to a single one of the résumés she'd mailed out.

Of course, she'd discovered yesterday that her phone wasn't working. No telling how long it had been out of service. No one could have reached her, even if they'd tried.

Cleo had had a plan when she left Chesapeake. Not a particularly well-thought-out plan, but a plan all the same.

Part of the trouble was that she'd never had an enormous amount of self-confidence, even before she'd married Niles. Some women were born knowing who they were, where they were going and how to get there. Not Cleo. She'd always been sort of hazy. A dreamer. An artist, to put a kinder face on it. And then, between Niles and her in-laws, what little self-confidence she'd once possessed had been systematically destroyed.

"Get moving, friend," she murmured. "Time's passing. Nothing's getting accomplished."

So she stretched, rubbed her back, savored another spoonful of rocky road and thought about names and about all the junk she'd found stashed away in various drawers, closets and Niles's wall safe. She'd started boxing it up, but what on earth was she going to do with it?

Thank goodness no one had inquired about the house. The rest of her life wasn't ready. Funny, no one had thought to tell her that pregnancy affected the brain.

Once the phone was back in service, she was going to have to get back on the ball, starting with her tire. Being alone and pregnant, miles from the nearest neighbor, with a flat tire and a phone out of service was no laughing matter. Not that she was laughing.

And of course, her tire hadn't been flat when she'd driven into town to report her phone out of order.

She sighed, licked off her ice-cream spoon and murmured, "Mabel." She'd known a Mabel once a long time ago. It was a nice name, but somehow it wasn't quite right.

Madelaine? Magnolia?

Magnolia, daughter of Niles and Cleopatra Barnes. Oh Lord, wouldn't her mother-in-law just love that?

Cleo scraped the bottom of the bowl, closed her eyes in a moment of ecstasy and considered going back for seconds.

Better not. She'd gained too much weight already. Either her hips had spread or the baby had dropped. She could barely waddle, and she still had six weeks to go.

"Marcia? Margaret?" She sampled the sound of two more names. Margaret was a pretty name. Old-fashioned. Nice and ordinary. After being christened Cleopatra Evangeline by a couple of hippy art students who'd been nowhere near ready to take on the responsibility of a family, she'd learned to appreciate nice, ordinary names.

Laying the name book facedown on a packing crate, Cleo eased herself awkwardly onto the leather-covered sofa and hoisted her legs one at a time. With a sigh, she placed both hands on her swollen stomach and closed her eyes.

Oh, shoot. Someone was at the door. Why couldn't he have come three minutes ago, before she'd sat down? She was tempted to pretend she didn't hear him, but it had to be the telephone repairman, and she needed the blasted phone.

She struggled to rise, a process that didn't grow easier with practice. The knock came again, and she grasped the back of the sofa and managed to get to her feet. "I'm coming, I'm coming," she grumbled, clasping a hand to her back.

Swinging the door wide, she said, "It's probably mice. They chewed through..." Her voice trailed off as she stared up at the large fist raised as if to knock again. Conditioned reflex took over before common sense could step in. Flinching, she flung up a protective hand.

"What the devil?" The man looked puzzled, not quite so threatening now that he'd lowered his fist.

Hormones. It had to be her crazy hormones, because she really wasn't paranoid. "I'm sorry." This was embarrassing. "You're not the telephone man, are you?"

"Do I look like a telephone man?"

He didn't. For one thing, he didn't have a name on his shirt. For another, she'd never seen a repairman dressed the way he was dressed, in casuals that cost more than her entire winter wardrobe. For still another, he had The Look.

Cleo knew all about The Look. She'd been drilled on it first by her late husband and then by her mother-in-law. It was what set The Haves, uppercase, apart from the have-nots, lowercase. It was the unspoken password, the subtle membership badge used by people like her in-laws to separate The Right People— again, uppercase—from the wrong people. Tiny, almost invisible lowercase.

She'd obviously been the wrong people.

Someone had introduced them at a party. She'd been wearing a borrowed scrap of sequined georgette and feeling worldly and beautiful. "You two have got to meet. Cleopatra, meet the Nile."

It had been Niles, not Nile. Close enough, though, after a few glasses of white wine. Their mutual friend had told them they were meant for each other, and Cleo, silly, romantic, impressionable fool that she was, had believed it.

They'd been married a week and a half later, after a whirlwind courtship. Before her honeymoon suntan had even faded, Niles had set about changing her into someone more acceptable to his parents.

Cleo blinked her way back to the present. "What do you want?" she demanded now, trying to sound more courteous than she felt.

"I saw the sign. I believe I'll take it."

"The sign?" She blinked again.

"The For Sale sign."

"You want my For Sale sign?"

He looked at her as if she were not quite bright. At the moment, she felt every bit as bright as a burned-out forty-watt bulb. "I want your house," he said patiently.

He didn't look quite as patient as he sounded. There was a twitch at one side of his jaw, a glint in his eyes that made her step back. Evidently, he took it as an invitation to enter and moved past her.

"Look, whoever you are, I don't—" she began, but he was too busy gazing up at the vaulted ceiling, at the moose head, the bear head, the coatrack made of antlers and all the rest of Niles's trophies. So she raised her voice. "I think you'd better go," she said firmly.

Evidently, the firmness didn't quite offset the faint quiver in her voice. The look he turned on her made her think of granite viewed through a layer of ice.

"I beg your pardon?" he countered mildly.

The massive rock fireplace, every rock trucked down from Virginia, had always struck her as slightly pretentious. He looked right at home standing there, under the mounted head of a black bear that was said to have been taken locally.

"I hate trophies," she said, and then was embarrassed because the remark was totally out of context. Not quite a month of living alone and she couldn't even carry on a coherent conversation.

"This is it," he said softly, almost reverently. Almost as out of context, but she knew what he meant. It was there in the possessive way he was gazing around her living room.

"No, it isn't." She crossed her arms, resting them on her protruding shelf. She wasn't exactly afraid, but it paid to be cautious. He was big. Not massive, but tall, lean and powerful. He didn't look particularly mean, but then, sometimes meanness didn't show until it was too late. Sometimes it was disguised by expensive clothes and nice manners and a smile that was...

She shivered in spite of the warmth of the early afternoon sun slanting through the windows. "I should have taken the sign down, but I forgot." He turned so quickly she flinched again, but held her ground. "You see, I've decided—"

"It's already sold?"

"Well, no, not exactly."

"Are you the owner? It's still for sale, then?"

"Yes, I am, and no, it's not. I told you, I've changed my mind."

"No, you didn't."

"Well, I would have if you'd given me a chance. This isn't a good time. For me, I mean. I'm, uh, I'm expecting a baby."

"I noticed," he said dryly.

She detected a slight thaw in those granite gray eyes. In an ordinary man it might even have passed for amusement. But he was no ordinary man, and she wasn't about to take chances.

Besides, if he was amused, it was at her expense, and that she could do without. "I'm sorry for your trouble. Driving all the way out here, I mean. Did the real estate agent send you? I need to call her as soon as I get the phones hooked up again. Anyway, I'm sure she'll be able to find you something else."

"But you see, I don't want something else," he explained gently, almost as if he were speaking to a child. "I want this place."

Harrison watched the words register and gauged their effect. She stared at him helplessly, her arms unconsciously cradling her bulging middle, anxiety and something that looked oddly like fear in her clear, honey-colored eyes.

She was a mess, he told himself. A genuine flake. Or maybe all pregnant women were this way. Never having been around one before, he couldn't say. But it wouldn't wash. She'd put her house up for sale and he'd decided to buy it. When it came to a straightforward business deal, he wasn't in the habit of backing down.

"What kind of a contract did you sign?"

She stared up at him in mute misery. He was almost tempted to back off, but then, he hadn't got where he was by backing off.

Wrong. That's precisely what got you where you are—the inability to back down from a challenge.

"Was it a thirty, sixty or ninety-day contract? How long ago did you sign it?"

"Five days ago," she whispered.

"Then the place is obviously still for sale. I've decided to buy it."

"But you haven't even seen it."

God, she really was a mess. Piles of straw-colored hair, half of it pinned up on top of her head, half spilling down over her shoulders. Clear brown eyes. Too clear. And a damned sight too revealing. Her chin was small, but she used it effectively. He summed up the parts and came up with the total.

Proud, determined and...vulnerable?

Vulnerable.

Oh, hell.

Reading the opposition was an art, one at which he excelled. Right now, he almost wished he didn't. "How much are you asking?"

A shadow flickered briefly in her eyes. He could practically hear the wheels spin. She would come up with a figure that was twice what she was really asking, thinking he'd turn it down and that would be the end of it.

She named a figure. It was half what he'd expected. Either the lady was loco or property values down here were at rock bottom. "Sold," he said, his voice devoid of the jubilation he was feeling.

Jubilation? Hell, you'd think he'd just pulled off a major coup instead of buying himself a log cabin that for all he knew was full of termites, damp rot and God knows what else on an unmarked dirt road in a jerkwater place that didn't even have a name. And all on an impulse that didn't even make sense.

"No, it's not sold," she snapped. "I told you I'd changed my mind. Look, I need to sit down. When I stand too long, all the iced tea I had for lunch runs down to my feet and ankles, and I can't get my shoes on."

Without waiting for a response, she plopped down onto the sofa.

Without waiting for an invitation, he took the matching chair. It fit him as if it had been custom designed for his six-foot, two-inch, one-hundred-and-ninety-seven-pound frame.

At least that's what he'd weighed when he'd gone into the hospital. Since then, subsisting on the boring diet prescribed by some witch doctor at the hospital and religiously followed right up to his last day in New York by his own chef, he was probably considerably less.

"Do you need to consult your husband first?"

"I don't have a husband."

He looked pointedly at her third finger, left hand. Following his gaze, she covered her bare fingers with her other hand.

"My fingers are too swollen to wear my rings, and anyway, it's none of your business whether or not I'm married."

"You're right. All the same, the place was obviously built and furnished by a man. I just assumed—"

"Well, don't."

He lifted both hands in a gesture of surrender.

Surrender, hell. Crazy or not, the place was beginning to grow on him. He had two other properties outside New York, both professionally decorated with custom-made furnishings and an art collection that had been chosen by a friend.

Chosen by an ex-lover, actually. She'd made a hell of a commission off him, too, not to mention all the gifts over the year and a half of their relationship.

He glanced at the window facing onto the river. "A van just pulled up out front."

She groaned and closed her eyes.

"Want me to handle it?"

He watched her struggle to rise, knew the exact moment when she surrendered to the inevitable. Her eyelids were shadowed. She looked tired. Tired and defeated, and vulnerable.

That word again. It made him feel uncomfortable. The women in his life were, without exception, about as vulnerable as sharks. He preferred strong, challenging women.

"Looks like the telephone company. Stay there, I'll show him in. If there's anything he needs to know, you can direct me from there."

So she did. Feeling guilty. Feeling like a coward for allowing a stranger to take over. She was just so tired. Her feet ached. She hadn't seen her anklebones in weeks. Her back hurt, and half the things she ate gave her heartburn. And now, in desperate need of relocation money, she had turned down the first offer she'd received for the lodge.

Or tried to turn it down.

Not even to herself would Cleo admit that for once, it was nice to leave things to someone else. Back in the early days of their marriage, she and Niles had decided to build a private hideaway somewhere within a day's drive of Richmond but well off the beaten track. It had been Niles who had chosen the architect. Niles who'd had final say on the design, who'd driven to High Point to select the furniture while she'd stayed behind to help his mother with one of her charity drives. She'd resented being left out, but by then she'd already been well on her way to becoming a doormat.

Niles had bought the trophies already mounted, claiming they'd impress the clients he intended to entertain here so that they could depreciate the lodge on their taxes.

Her watercolors, the ones she'd done when they'd vacationed here between clients, had been relegated to one of the guest rooms. She'd been allowed to furnish only one wing—two small bedrooms and a bath. Mrs. Barnes, on her one and only visit, had criticized Cleo's taste in decor as well as her ability as a watercolorist. In retaliation, Cleo had dashed off a scathing caricature of the older woman.

Of course, she'd ripped it up immediately, but it had given her a small sense of power that had lasted until they'd returned to Richmond, to the huge Victorian mansion they shared with Niles's parents.

Now, lying on the vast leather-covered sofa, which was hot and sticky against her bare skin, she sighed, listening absently to the low rumble of masculine voices from the kitchen area.

It was probably a mess. She'd started to make a sandwich, changed her mind and dipped a bowlful of ice cream instead. And then he'd shown up. She didn't even know his name.

Not that it mattered. Not that anything seemed to matter much lately. She spent half her time traipsing back and forth to the bathroom, the other half floating along on a dreamy mirage, just as if everything were under control.

Nothing was under control. In six weeks she was going to have a baby. She no longer had a home, much less a job. She'd left Richmond to move in with a friend without telling her in-laws she was pregnant because they would have taken over her life and her baby. Niles's baby. And wrong or not, she couldn't bear to move back into that stately mausoleum, her every thought subject to Vesper's approval.

Vesper Barnes was the kind of woman who, if she met God face-to-face, would have looked down her nose and asked Him who His people were, and if they weren't among the First Families of Virginia, heaven help Him.

Niles's father, Henry, was even worse. He had to be in control. What he couldn't control, he destroyed. In the end, he had destroyed his son by demanding that Niles be someone he was incapable of being.

"All done," Granite Eyes said, coming in from the adjoining kitchen.

Cleo blinked up at him. For a large man, he moved too quietly. "Thank you. How much do I owe?"

"No charge."

"Certainly there's a charge. Oh—I suppose it'll show up on my phone bill."

"There's food out on the table. Would you like me to do something with it?"

"Would I like *what?*" She struggled to sit up.

His smile was a work of art, but he wasn't taking her in with it. She'd been taken in by experts. "It looks like I interrupted your lunch," he said.

"You didn't. Thank you for taking care of the phone thing. Drive carefully." When he didn't react, she added, "Have a nice day," and felt even more like a fool.

With his long-fingered hands bracing narrow hips, he reminded her of a pirate ruling from his poop deck, or wherever it was pirates ruled their ships from.

"You're not going to leave, are you?" She experienced a sinking feeling, more like resignation than fear.

Neither of them said a word about the lodge. About the contract she'd signed with the real estate people and whether or not he could force her to honor it. Her stomach churned. Now even ice cream was giving her heartburn.

Well...shoot.

He just smiled. Stood there in his expensive shoes, with his thumbs hooked into the hip pockets of his expensive pants, and smiled.

And she lay there in her mail-order tent dress, with her bare, swollen feet propped on a red-and-white cowhide pillow, and burst into tears.

Two

That night in his motel room, Harrison considered checking out and heading back to New York. It had been a long, eventful day and he was tired.

After years of chauffeured limousines and private jets, he had quickly come to enjoy being in control of a powerful, well-engineered vehicle, free to go when and where he pleased. The sense of freedom was new.

The urge to control was not. But it was one of the things he was working on. Learning to ease up. To let go. To relax, if he had to do it one muscle, one gray cell at a time.

Cutting down hadn't worked. He'd tried limiting his hours, but there was no way he could shut off his brain. He'd drawn the line at meditation, yoga and biofeedback. One of his personal assistants had suggested aromatherapy, whatever the hell that was.

He'd spent three weeks examining his options, and then he'd placed a call to the West Coast, to a highly innovative competitor who had approached him two years before about a possible merger. He'd laid out his terms. They'd spent a month negotiating and arrived at a mutually satisfactory deal with a minimum of hassle. The details had been left to their respective legal departments and directors.

He'd been able to block off second thoughts right up until the end, but then it had struck him. Now that he had been relieved of any possible source of stress, what the devil was he supposed to do with the rest of his life? Hang out in Central Park feeding the pigeons?

He'd made himself get on with the tedious business of dividing his assets among various trusts, endowments, annuities and a few large charitable bequests. Under the circumstances he figured it couldn't hurt to be on the right side of the angels.

By the time he'd headed south, there was only one loose end that hadn't been taken care of. Marla.

Marla Kane, good friend, ex-lover. She'd been out of town when he'd left, and he couldn't deny he'd been relieved. Funny how a man who made business decisions involving hundreds of millions of dollars on the basis of a hunch could go to such lengths to avoid making certain personal decisions.

Although he was improving on that score. The decision to buy the log house was personal. A snap decision based solely on instinct. But then, what was instinct besides a knack for absorbing information subliminally and reaching a conclusion? Nine times out of ten, his instincts were right on target. In the rare instance when he was wrong, he cut his losses, analyzed his mistakes and, as a consequence, never made the same one twice.

He hoped to hell this wasn't going to be one of those learning experiences.

Standing before the open window of his riverside motel, he watched the stars come out and thought about snap decisions in general, about today's decision in particular. And about the woman.

Her name was Cleo Barnes. Something about her intrigued him, and Harrison couldn't remember the last time he'd been intrigued by a woman. Much less by a woman like Ms. Barnes, who was not only pregnant and untidy, but about as sharp-witted as a bowling ball.

Fortunately, she wasn't part of the deal. If at some time in the future he changed his mind about the house, he could always put it back on the market. A house was a commodity, no more, no less.

As for the woman, she wasn't quite as easy to classify. Something about her didn't add up. He probably should have hung around, at least until she'd calmed down. She'd started to cry. He'd panicked. He'd felt obligated to do something, or at least say something, but was afraid anything he did or said short of bowing out completely might be construed as taking advantage of an opponent's weakness.

But what if she was in some kind of trouble? A woman didn't burst into tears for no reason, did she?

He hated tears. He was always embarrassed when a woman cried. Emotions, especially the messier emotions, were either a sign of weakness or a signal that the woman wanted something from him.

On the other hand, for a woman in her condition, it could have been a simple matter of hormones.

All the same, he'd been embarrassed, so instead of trying to comfort her, he'd found her a box of tissues, mumbled something about not seeing him out and left her there on the sofa.

Left her pregnant, alone and crying. Closing his

mind to all that, he had driven straight to the real estate office, signed an option to buy and felt guilty as hell all the way back to the motel.

"What the devil have you done to feel guilty about?" he muttered. The house was for sale. He was buying it. End of story.

It had to be this crazy diet he'd been halfheartedly trying to follow. Cutting out everything that made life worthwhile was bound to affect a man's thought processes.

He removed a cigar from the case in his jacket pocket, inhaled the rich aroma of Cuban tobacco and put it away again. How the devil could he kick back and enjoy his one cigar of the day when he kept seeing her the way she'd looked when she'd first opened the door, her face tanned, flushed and innocent of makeup. Before she could utter a single word, the look in those clear brown eyes had told him two things.

One—she was frightened. And two—he was about as welcome as a bad case of food poisoning.

Once inside, he'd considered offering her one of his business cards by way of introduction, but decided against it because it no longer defined his identity. As for his new identity, that was a work in progress.

He took out the cigar again. This time he clipped the end, lighted it and took one draw, blowing out a cloud of aromatic smoke before stubbing it out.

The process of redefining his identity had actually begun a couple of years ago, when he'd received a letter informing him that he was one of several heirs to an undivided tract of land somewhere in northeastern North Carolina. In a battle to fight off a hostile takeover at the time, he'd turned over the letter to his personal lawyer and promptly dismissed it from his mind.

Not until a few months later, when he was flat on his back in a hospital bed, hooked up to a bank of monitoring machines and wondering if he would ever walk out of there alive, had he given the matter a second thought.

On being told that unless he wanted to die at an even earlier age than his father had, he was going to have to make some drastic changes, he'd come face-to-face with his own mortality.

It had scared the hell out of him.

"Is this everything you know about your medical history?" his cardiologist had asked, scanning his notes. "A few broken bones, sports related. The usual childhood stuff. Hmm, insomnia, tension headaches, occasional dyspepsia—that's it? No vices?"

"No more than you'd expect in a man my age. I don't take chances, if that's what you mean."

"Good. Then I take it you don't smoke, don't drink—"

"Cigars. I like a good cigar after meals."

"Cut down to one and then phase it out. Drink?"

"Not a lot. Actually, more beer than anything else."

"Better not. New study out. Switch to red wine, but don't overdo it. Your cholesterol's pushing four hundred. Your blood pressure's a time bomb waiting to go off. I'm going to put you on medication for the time being, but I'd like to see you tackle this thing another way. So tell me, what kind of exercise do you do?"

Thoroughly disgruntled but scared enough to hear the man out, he'd stuck pretty close to the truth. "I used to ski. Haven't had time lately. I was on the swimming team in my undergrad days. Now it's mostly walking." With a tendency to pace and an office the size of a gymnasium, he figured he got in enough mileage to qualify as exercise.

"What about genetics? Anybody in your family other than your father have a history of heart problems?"

"My father didn't have a history, he had a single heart attack and died."

"At age forty-seven, I believe you said. And you're...what? Ah, thirty-seven. Right. Well, son, I'm going to send a dietitian in to talk to you about your diet, among other things. Meanwhile..."

Meanwhile, he'd been poked, prodded, explored and wired up like a Christmas tree. He'd been warned against everything that gave life meaning and released with orders to unload a lifetime accumulation of stress and learn how to relax.

Once released, he'd gone home, taken the phones off the hook, given orders that he wasn't to be disturbed and locked himself in his study. He'd clipped a cigar and left it unlit, poured himself a drink and left it untouched. He had stared out at the familiar skyline until the first streaks of dawn began to dim Manhattan's glitter. Grudgingly, reluctantly, he had faced his choices. He could sell out and leave town, or he could hang around the same scene, seeing the same people, and try to modify his behavior. He'd never been good at compromise, at half measures, but he could give it a shot.

Less than a week later, one of his closest friends had dropped dead in the middle of a board meeting. Suddenly, all the warnings he'd been given had hit home. That was when he'd set the wheels in motion.

It was the questions about his medical history that had first touched off a mild curiosity concerning his inheritance. Family had never been more than an abstract concept. He'd grown up as the only child of a distant, overachieving father and a neurotic mother, and when he'd thought of family at all, it had been as something to avoid whenever possible. It had simply never occurred to him to wonder what sort of people he'd sprung from. Whether or not any of them had blue-gray eyes and a tendency to chronic insomnia. Whether or not any of them liked Mexican beer and Cuban cigars. If any of them had been allergic to champagne or cashew nuts.

Acting on impulse, he'd sent Perry Edwards, one of his three personal assistants, to North Carolina with instructions to locate the property, check out the possibilities and get back to him ASAP.

The first report hadn't been long in coming. Timber. Large presence in area by major producer. Also corn, cotton, soybeans and potatoes. Possibly other crops. No industry.

Since he'd invested in timber, cotton and soybeans on the commodities market, his interest had perked up. The report also mentioned a dwelling located somewhere on the property.

He'd filed the information away in the back of his mind while he wound up his affairs. By the time he'd headed south, his mind was already working on plans, contingency plans and backup plans.

He wasn't exactly sure which plan he was working on now.

On day one he had checked into the motel Perry had recommended and spent hours poring over surveys, tax maps and old deeds. A few of the deeds, written in the descriptive style of the period, had read almost like an old diary.

On day two he'd hired a guide to show him over his legacy. By the time he'd returned to the motel, he'd been tired, discouraged, all but ready to admit defeat. It seemed that his legacy, while it might once have included hundreds of acres of valuable timber and farmland, had shrunk over the years. After previous generations skimmed off the gravy, and various green groups condemned large portions for the sake of whatever wildlife happened to live there, all that was left was swamp.

If there was a commercial use for swampland, it had yet to be discovered.

As for the house, it was little more than a ruin. Whatever elements of grandeur it might once have possessed had long since fallen victim to time, mud and generations of hunters and trappers who used it as a convenient camp.

At least he now knew who he was and what kind of people he had sprung from. The surveyor, a character called Catfish who fancied himself a raconteur, had regaled Harrison with a detailed history of dozens of previous Lawlesses. It seemed his father's heritage was somewhat less than illustrious. No wonder he'd never mentioned it. Moonshiners? Felons? Bigamists?

Harrison had fully intended to leave the next morning, but for some reason, he hadn't. Instead, he'd started thinking about all those earlier Lawlesses who had grown up in the area. Most had been farmers. A few had been fishermen or guides. There'd been a couple of boat builders and a state senator. One Lawless had died in prison, another had gone into law.

And one—his own father—had founded a small investment house and a major chain of resort hotels.

Learning that he was a direct descendant, several generations removed, of a man whose given name was Squire Lawless, who had operated an illicit distillery right in the middle of the ancestral acres, took some getting used to. He'd always assumed, if he'd thought about it at all, that he was a product of generations of men just like his father.

Evidently, there was a strong strain of ambition in the Lawless stock. Old Squire had been an entrepreneur, and a damned successful one, from all he'd been able to discover. There'd been a few notable failures over the past generations, but Harrison thought on the whole, the old man had passed on some pretty potent genes.

He wondered if his own father would have felt the same way. King had believed in following both the letter and the spirit of every law on the books. It was a wonder he'd been as successful as he had, in today's business climate. Harrison would like to think he'd inherited the best from both men. Time would tell.

Meanwhile, he had some time to kill.

Fully intending to head north again, he'd found himself walking around the small, sleepy town of Columbia, built in a curve of the winding Scuppernong River, with a tiny marina, hundred-year-old cottages and turn-of-the-century gingerbread homes.

He had spent the entire day exploring, unconsciously absorbing the slower pace of life. On the way back to the motel, tired, hungry, but more relaxed than he could remember being in years, he'd followed his nose and ended up at a barbecue place. Before he'd remembered the doctor's orders, he was halfway through a plate of the best barbecue he'd ever tasted.

Sated, he'd gone back to his room, smoked a cigar and decided that moderation made more sense than austerity. Cutting down, not out. A moderate diet. A moderate program of exercise. Walking, maybe even running, but no competitive sports. No more of his favorite Mexican beer. Beer, it seemed, was contraindicated for heart patients.

Wine, then. He could live with a decent cabernet.

East Carolina barbecue was lean pork. Pork was white meat. He could live with that if he had to.

Meanwhile, the natives seemed friendly. On reflection, he'd decided he could do a lot worse than hang around here in the land of his beginnings until he decided what to do with the rest of his life.

Not that he hadn't had plenty of offers before he'd even left the hospital. He'd been invited to spend as much time as he needed recuperating on a certain ranch out in New Mexico. Ditto a villa in the south of France. Ditto a cozy palazzo in Florence.

The trouble was, all the offers had come from women with whom he'd been involved at one time or another, and all came with strings attached. Even at death's door, he was considered prime husband material, thanks in large part to a monthly piece in *Prominence Magazine* naming him one of the world's most eligible bachelors.

What was it they'd called him? The pirate prince?

He was no pirate. Not that he didn't know a few. Professional CEOs who moved from company to company, skimming off profits, looting assets, moving on to the next victim. But he wasn't among them. He liked to think of himself as a builder, not a plunderer.

As for being a prince, while it was true that his father, Kingston Lancaster Lawless, called King by his enemies and even his few friends, had inherited a few million and parlayed it into billions before dying of a massive coronary, the analogy ended there. King had left a rich widow who'd gone through the motions of grieving for all of three weeks and a son who'd been determined not to follow in his father's footsteps.

Or at least not to ride his father's coattails.

Instead, he had transferred from Harvard to MIT, earned a couple of degrees and built his own empire, and now, here he was, starting all over again.

Somehow, the idea didn't seem quite as discouraging as it had only a few days ago. The barbecue had helped. So had being free to drive as long and as far as he liked, with no deadlines, no boundaries—no secretaries reminding him of meetings, commitments, appointments.

Feeling relaxed and energized at the same time, Harrison stretched out on the motel bed, which was both too small and too hard, and began revising his plan of action.

First on the list: buy the lodge. That was already in the works. He'd agreed to the asking price and the house was now under option—to him. He was pretty sure Ms. Barnes wouldn't have the legal gumption to contest the signed contract. And he wasn't going to point out the legal possibilities to her.

Next item: send for the things he'd put in storage. Better yet, find out from the Realtor what furnishings, if any, were included with the sale and then fill in with whatever was needed. As long as he had a king-size bed with a good mattress and a place to set up his computers, the rest could wait.

Next on the list: hire a housekeeper-cook. The doctor had said simplify. He'd said nothing about starving in squalor.

On to Marla. Item four. He would call and invite her down to look over the house. Ever since he'd left the hospital, he'd been reading up on stress reduction. In the process he'd learned that married men had a far greater survival rate. The statistics alone were enough to triple the marriage rate and wipe out divorce altogether. Divorced men, according to one expert, were twenty-one times more likely to enter psychiatric hospitals. Their death rate was twice as high for heart disease, four times as high for pneumonia and seven times as high for suicide.

Ergo, the need for a reliable, stress-free wife. Of all the women with whom he'd been involved, Marla was the best candidate. She was intelligent, resourceful and beautiful. She wasn't tied down to a career in New York. If she was hardly the most exciting bed partner he'd ever had, all the better. Too much excitement was probably bad for a man in his condition.

Mental note: find out about risks involved with sex.

Marla had a son from her first marriage. Richard...Robert... Something with an *R*, anyway. Harrison had never met the boy, who spent most of his time either away at school or with his father, but that was no problem. Children were number five on his list. A son first. A daughter approximately three years later, if all went well. With little Radley or whatever, that would give him his allotted two-point-something-or-other children.

Mental note: have a personal assistant check out schools in area.

Mental note: man, you don't have a PA. You're on your own now, remember?

So be it.

He yawned. A good sign. All in all, he felt pretty damned good about the whole crazy situation. It was sheer coincidence, the way things had turned out. The legacy, which he'd all but forgotten. The coronary, which had precipitated a drastic change in his lifestyle. The fact that the house on the property he'd inherited was uninhabitable. The fact that, with time on his hands and nothing better to do, he'd spent a day exploring the area.

The fact that he'd happened to turn off onto an unmarked road, happened to glance up at the right moment, happened to notice the For Sale sign....

Pure coincidence, nothing more than that. He'd once read some statistics on coincidences. It seemed they happened far more frequently than was generally thought.

Interesting, he mused, and yawned again.

On with his agenda. Next item: prying a pregnant woman out of her nest. Not something he looked forward to doing, but it had to be done, for her own good. She'd been the one to put the place on the market, after all. Which meant she either wanted to sell or needed to sell or both. If she was having second thoughts now, it was probably because he'd caught her at a bad time.

Or maybe it was just a pregnant-woman thing. Like pickles and ice cream.

Whatever her problem was, he could afford to take it slow and easy now that he'd signed that option and handed over the good faith money. Timing was everything. He was in no hurry.

Next item...

Mid-agenda, Harrison Lawless, insomniac ex-tycoon, drifted off to sleep.

Cleo was in the shower the next morning when someone pounded on the front door. Whoever it was had probably been knocking for ages. With the water running, she hadn't been able to hear.

Might not have answered even if she'd heard. She still hadn't gotten over yesterday's encounter, when she'd been forced to come to terms with reality.

Hastily, she blotted her face and those parts of her body she could still reach, then slipped on a faded denim tent dress and padded barefoot to the front door.

"Sorry. I didn't mean to disturb you." He was leaning against the door frame, silhouetted against the glare of sun glinting off the water.

Inhaling the scent of freshly laundered cotton and a brisk aftershave, she stepped back. She'd been expecting him. Dreading it, wanting only to slip back into her nice, safe cocoon. Knowing she was caught in a trap of her own making.

The agency had called yesterday to tell her they had a sale for the lodge, and it was a sure thing. The buyer had accepted every single one of her terms. After hanging up, she had cried some more, and then cursed, and then cleaned out the last of the rocky road. None of it had helped.

"You didn't disturb me," she said with a sigh. "You might as well come in...."

Three

Harrison allowed his opponent to take the lead. As a tactic, it was often advantageous. It took her a few tries, but once she hit her stride, he sat back and let her run, confident of the outcome.

She shot him an accusing look. "Tell me the truth, you wanted to buy my house no matter what I was asking for it, didn't you?"

"Your asking price is reasonable."

"Yes, but you didn't know that. Besides, it's got mice."

He nodded thoughtfully.

"And—and maybe even termites. Well, maybe not termites. I think Niles had an exterminator, but I'm pretty sure there're a few powder post beetles. It takes centuries for them to eat up a house, but even so…and there's only one nest of mice. And with cross ventilation, I don't even have to run the air conditioner until July."

Bless her little heart, didn't she realize what she was doing? The more she talked, the more she undermined her own position. It was enough like taking candy from a baby to make him feel mildly guilty, but not enough to change his mind.

"Mrs. Dunn at the agency said she'd never even

heard of you before you walked in yesterday afternoon and said you'd take it.''

He waited. Not a tense bone in his body. Piece of cake.

"You did it deliberately, knowing I had changed my mind.''

"So you said. I don't believe we settled it yesterday. There was the matter of your contract? Giving the Realtor the ability to okay a deal?''

She nodded slowly, then frowned. It occurred to him that even when she was scowling at him, her face had a glowing, dew-kissed look that no amount of cosmetics could have achieved. Conditioned to avoid anything that could possibly be construed as sexual harassment, he refrained from mentioning it.

"I believe you said you listed the place five days ago.'' His gaze fell to her belly. The inference was clear. "May I ask why you left it until the last minute?''

"No, you may not,'' she snapped, and then told him anyway. "My baby's not due for six weeks. That's plenty of time. It—it took longer than I expected to clear up the estate.''

The estate. He lifted an eyebrow, silently encouraging her to explain. Husband? Father?

Husband. She was a widow, he'd lay odds on it.

He murmured something that could conceivably be taken for sympathy and waited. Ten seconds. Twenty. Right on the count of thirty, she took a deep breath, throwing certain portions of her anatomy into further prominence. "Yes, well, you see…''

He'd thought big, really huge, when he'd seen that yellow nightgown on the clothesline. But except for one area, she wasn't a large woman. Small bones. Hands and feet that were probably long and narrow under normal conditions. At the moment they were a bit puffy.

She was saying, "You'd think a lawyer would have known better. I guess he thought he was too young to have a will, but even so…"

Even so, Harrison prompted silently. Come on, lady, cut to the chase.

"Well, there was the prenuptial agreement. But of course, the lodge is marital property."

He nodded gravely. "Of course."

"It's just that everything takes so much longer than I expected."

"By everything, I take it you're not talking about your, uh, the baby."

"Not the baby. My résumés and all this." She waved a hand in the general direction of several half-filled cartons scattered around the room.

Don't ask, Lawless. If she starts making sense, just get the hell out.

"Things just sort of slipped up on me, and now I'm not sure I'll have time to finish what I started. Sorting everything out, deciding what I want and what I don't, packing it all up and then finding another place to move into. It's not as simple as it sounds. And besides, there's a mallard nesting near a pond behind the house, and I have to try and guard her against snakes."

That's it. He started to rise and make his excuses. Ducks and beetles he could live with. Even mice. Snakes he didn't even want to hear about.

"They eat eggs and baby ducks, you know. Well,

of course, snakes have to eat, too, but I've been watching that nest ever since I've been here, and I'm pretty sure she's the same duck that used to nest in the same spot back when—'' She sighed, momentarily looking as if her train of thought had been derailed, and then she managed to get it back on track again. "Well, anyway, I couldn't bear it if something happened to her babies while I was here to prevent it.''

Harrison settled back into the chair. Sorting chaff from wheat, he selected a promising nugget. "You don't live here full-time, then?''

"Certainly not. I haven't been here in nearly three years, which is probably why the place was such a mess. We used to come several times a year, but Niles—that is, my husband—needed it more and more for business.''

"I see,'' murmured Harrison, seeing all sorts of things she'd probably prefer him not to see. Things she might not see herself.

"Well, anyway, now you understand why I can't sell it just now.''

"Because you're afraid a snake will eat some eggs.''

"You're being deliberately obtuse, Mr. Lawless. I am not—''

"Harrison. And it's Chloe, isn't it?'' He knew exactly what her name was. It had been on the option he'd signed.

"It's Cleo! And I didn't change my mind because of a snake, I changed my mind because there's a lot more to do than I expected, and because I have to think about what to keep and what to throw away—

what's important and what's not—and all of it takes time and energy and I'm running out of both, and there's a lot of bending involved, which I don't do so well anymore.''

She shoved her hair out of her face. On anyone else, her expression might be called pugnacious. With a heart-shaped face, a pair of lucent brown eyes and a soft, vulnerable mouth, it was...

Something other than that.

Her cheeks were flushed. She was breathing hard. ''Are you all right?'' he asked, suddenly uneasy. He leaned forward to touch her face. She looked feverish.

Judging from the way she flinched, she was as startled by the gesture as he was. It wasn't the sort of thing he did as a rule. Touching. Certainly not with strangers.

''I'm fine,'' she said, but obviously she wasn't. She sounded tired and discouraged. ''I think it must be the heat. I never turn on the AC in May, but maybe just this once...'' She bit her lip, drawing attention to it. Harrison shifted uncomfortably. ''And I'm not sleeping well, either. I can't seem to stop thinking at night, and I can't seem to focus on anything during the day, and—'' She broke off with a rueful smile. ''I'm whining, aren't I? I can't stand people who whine. I never used to do it, but then, I never used to run out of energy, either. Lately all I seem to want to do is lie in the hammock on the back deck and watch the birds.''

Harrison knew all about escape, all about denial. He also knew that denying a fact didn't change it. ''Boat watching from the front deck, bird watching from the back. I'll probably be doing both once I move in.''

''You're not moving in.''

He didn't bother to argue. It wasn't necessary. All he had to do was give her enough rope.

''Look, I already told you I've changed my mind. I'm nowhere near ready to move out.''

''I'm afraid it's not that simple,'' he said gently. ''Let's see if we can't negotiate a—''

A mutually satisfactory arrangement, he was going to say, when she flung out her hands, grimaced and clutched her swollen sides. Alarm bells went off in his mind. *Don't go into labor on me, lady. Don't fight dirty.*

''Is there, uh, a problem?'' He indicated her lump. Her pregnancy? What the devil did you call the thing at this stage?

She caught her breath and then smiled. ''She's going to be a ballet dancer. They have to start training early.''

''Is there someone you can call?''

''I don't need to call anyone. I told you, I'm not due for another six weeks.''

''Six weeks sounds like enough time for us to get things settled between us.'' He leaned back again in the large oak-and-leather chair and waited for the next move. This was hardly the first time he'd dealt with a woman on a matter of business. Some of them were sharper than their male counterparts, possibly because they'd had to be to get where they were.

This one, though, was totally outside his experience, both businesswise and otherwise. He didn't know how to handle her. She didn't react the way any sensible woman would react. Against all reason, he found himself relishing the challenge.

He tried a diversionary tactic. "Does the fireplace draw?"

"The fireplace? Oh, um... Well, it used to. I suppose it still does. Did you ask at the agency about other properties? I'm pretty sure Mrs. Dunn can find something with a wonderful fireplace. Maybe even something on the beach. Had you thought about that? A beach cottage, a fireplace...lovely."

Oh, hell. So much for diversionary tactics. "Thanks, but I've already found what I'm looking for." He waited for the message to hit home. She didn't need stress any more than he did. What she needed, he told himself, was a hassle-free sale so that she could go somewhere and have her baby, free of mice, snakes, ducks and termites. Actually, he was doing her a big favor by not letting her wiggle out of the contract.

"Ms. Barnes, you don't seem to appreciate the fact that I'm doing you a favor. I've agreed to your asking price. I've agreed to your terms. I'll pay whatever additional costs are involved."

Her eyes snapped open again. She glared at him. "And that's another thing—why didn't you try to bargain? What kind of man just walks in off the street like that?"

One, two, three, four, five.... Take a deep breath, Lawless, you're on the home stretch. "I saw your sign, remember? If you'd put up a No Trespassing sign instead of a For Sale sign, I wouldn't be here." Having regained the advantage, he watched her take in the words and mull them over. Pucker of brows, gnawing of lower lip. "Cleo?" he prodded gently when a full minute had passed with no comeback.

"Where was I? Oh, yes—what kind of man just strolls in out of the blue and says, I'll take it, without even asking the price? And you didn't, did you? You said you'd take it before I even told you how much I wanted, and that's crazy! You shouldn't do that. I might have come down on the price, for all you know."

"Would you have come down?"

She picked at a loose thread on her pocket. She was wearing faded blue denim that lent her skin an incandescent glow. "Maybe. I don't know. I suppose it depends on whether you'd shown up right after they put up the sign, before I decided not to sell."

"The thing is, you didn't take down the sign. You didn't notify your agent you'd changed your mind." Her gaze slid away and he pressed his advantage. "Tell me something, Cleo, do you know the ramifications of signing a contract?"

"My husband was a lawyer. My father-in-law is a lawyer. My uncle-in-law is a lawyer. Of course I know about contracts."

"And yet you're willing to risk a breach-of-contract suit on a mere whim?" As if he would take things that far.

"It's not mere, and it's certainly not a whim! It's— I simply can't—oh, why don't you just disappear?"

"Better yet, why don't I go fix us something cold to drink? You look like you could use a refresher. Juice? Milk?"

"Well...maybe a glass of iced tea." She was horizontal again. He knew her pattern now. Sit, then lean, then ease one leg up and then the other...and then close her eyes, cross her hands over her belly and sigh.

He also knew that with her center of gravity as distorted as it was, she had a hard time getting up again. "Iced tea sounds perfect. How about something to eat? Did you have breakfast yet?"

"I had some ice cream."

Levering himself easily out of the deep, oversize chair, Harrison headed for the kitchen and paused to glance over his shoulder. "Breakfast is important. You're eating for two now, remember?"

God, would you look who's spouting platitudes. Was this what happened when a man was forced to give up beer and red meat and settle for pasta and red wine?

"What are you, a doctor?" she muttered. "Some kind of a health nut?"

"Everybody's a health nut these days, to some degree or other. I believe it's a government mandate. Now, how about some cereal?"

"With ice cream on it?"

He winced. "Why not?"

"Left side's the freezer, cereal's in the third cabinet on the right over the chopping block." She managed to look anxious and eager at the same time. He wished she wouldn't. It made him feel like a brute. "Bowls are in the dishwasher. I think they're done, but I'm not certain. Yell if you can't find a clean one."

He ought to be ashamed of himself, using food to undermine her defenses. Not that he hadn't wined and dined his share of women with a view to, in the vernacular, having his way with them.

But this was different. Sex wasn't even a consideration. The woman was not only extremely pregnant, she was a certified ditz. A disorganized, unsophisticated flake in dire need of a keeper.

Funny how a man could suddenly come face-to-face with his true nature when he least expected it. Maybe that pirate business hadn't been so far off track, after all.

Harrison took down both boxes and scanned the labels. The dietitian had advised him what to look out for. Brown-sugar-added versus honey-dipped. Here we go, apples, dates and nuts. Nuts were fat but unsaturated. Fruit was good. Eat enough of the right stuff and you live forever, barring traffic accidents.

"Help yourself if you're hungry," Cleo called out from the next room.

He picked out a fragment of varnished pecan, tasted it and shuddered. And then he spied the coffeemaker, red light beckoning, pot still more than half-full.

She probably shouldn't be drinking the stuff, but there was no reason why *he* shouldn't. *He* wasn't pregnant.

He carried her breakfast in on a tray and helped her into a sitting position, trying not to react to the scent of soap, shampoo and talcum power, and then he headed back to the kitchen for his coffee.

Talcum powder? An *aphrodisiac?*

No way. That part of his anatomy was evidently as screwed up as everything else.

Filling a mug with reheated coffee, he strolled back

into the living room in time to see her lick her spoon and roll her eyes. An assortment of impressions kicked in. He dismissed them as irrelevant, not to mention highly inappropriate.

"Feeling better now?" he queried with the kind of heavy-handed cheeriness he'd come to despise during his convalescence.

"Mmm." She smiled. It was the first genuine smile she'd offered him. For about half a beat it threw him off stride, which was probably the reason he scowled at her.

Or maybe it was the coffee that made him scowl. It was weak, flat, scorched and decaffeinated. "Then let's get down to brass tacks, shall we?"

"Let's don't."

Calmly, he took out the checkbook he'd brought along, uncapped his pen and waited. *Dangle the bait and wait, Lawless, don't try to flog the poor fish to death with it.*

An assortment of emotions flickered across her face, and he thought there ought to be a law against eyes that revealing.

"You're not supposed to pay me, are you? I think you're supposed to arrange all that with a bank, or at least do it with the agent. I've never done this before."

"Naturally, I'll go through the agency. We can handle this any way you want. Lump sum—there'll be tax implications, of course—or monthly payments? Annual payments with adjustable rates? Fixed rates? Your choice." He smiled, hoping he didn't look as much like a shark as he felt. "I just thought a little extra earnest money up front might come in handy, with the baby coming so soon.''

You're a low-down, dirty rat, Lawless. That's really hitting below the belt.

He was right, though. She was worried about money. Some women needed help managing their business affairs, others didn't. At a time like this, Cleo Barnes obviously shouldn't be trying to do it all alone. Her father-in-law was a lawyer. Why wasn't he looking after her business interests? Maybe he should suggest it.

And maybe he should shut up. If her timing was lousy, that was no fault of his. He was a businessman and this was a straightforward business deal. She had something he wanted; she'd put it on the market; he'd agreed to buy. End of story.

''Could I have some more?'' She held out her bowl. He had a feeling duck watching wasn't her only means of escapism. Ice cream evidently ran a close second.

''There's not much left in the carton. Why not save it for lunch? We need to get matters settled between us so you can get on with your packing and I can get the ball rolling.'' He hated red tape. Over the years he'd waded through enough of the stuff to circle the globe.

Or rather, his legal department had. He was coming to realize just how many things he'd taken for granted.

Cleo placed her empty bowl on the cluttered coffee table beside his untouched coffee mug, wishing she could at least have offered him a decent cup of coffee.

Hers was pretty bad. It was one of the things Niles used to complain about.

For God's sake, Cleo, can't you do anything right? I knew you were no rocket scientist when I married you, but any dunce can learn to make a decent cup of coffee!

Remembering, she felt the old familiar burning in her esophagus. It had started about a year into her marriage, gotten better when they'd separated, worse when she'd come back, and better again, to her everlasting shame, after Niles had been killed.

Now it was back. This time it wasn't fear, it was nature's way of telling her she'd screwed up again.

"I'll have to drive into town. I'm almost out of bread, too."

"Fine. We can stop in at the agency and sign whatever needs signing while we're at it."

"We're not going anywhere. I am. If you want to leave your name and address with the agent, she can get in touch with you when I'm ready to sell if you still haven't found anything."

Harrison allowed her a few moments to savor her triumph before he played his ace. "Is that your car with the flat tire?"

At her stricken look, he nearly relented. "I can call a garage for you. They probably charge by the mile. What is it, about fifteen, twenty miles? I guess that's just one of the trade-offs for living so far out in the country."

Cleo hauled herself to a sitting position again, wishing pregnancy wasn't so darned undignified. "I do know how to change a tire."

"I'm sure you do."

"I happen to have three-fourths of a college degree, and until three weeks ago I held an excellent position with one of the better galleries in Virginia."

Her three-fourths of a degree was in art. Her excellent position was as a glorified gofer. The gallery was a tiny hole-in-the-wall place that barely paid enough to live on, and no benefits at all. Even if she wanted to go back to Chesapeake, she'd have to find a better job, and so far, not a single one of her résumés had drawn a response.

"Well, say something," she snapped. "I know what you're thinking. You think I'm one of those helpless women who can't do anything for herself. For your information, I'm perfectly capable of taking care of myself. I've been doing it for years. I expect to go on doing it, so thanks for the offer, but no thanks."

He waited until the steam cleared. Waited to see if she had anything more to say on the subject. She usually did, and it was the addendum that was most revealing.

"It just so happens that I haven't gotten around to fixing my flat tire, but it's not because I don't know how."

"I'm sure it's not," Harrison murmured. "Look, I have in mind a deal that might save us both some inconvenience."

He'd thought it over the night before. Never go in without a plan, a backup plan and a fall-back plan, that was his motto.

Tilting her head, she sent him a suspicious look. Before she could launch another attack, he said, "As long as we're going into town anyway, you might as well clean out the last of the ice cream.''

Offering her a smile worthy of one of the world's most eligible bachelors, he left her there on the sofa, one leg up, one down, both hands on her belly and a look of sheer frustration on her face.

"So, here's the deal,'' he said a few minutes later, handing over a bowlful of rocky road, premium-grade, high-fat ice cream with a generous drench of chocolate syrup on top. As a bribe, it couldn't begin to compare with his usual offering, especially as it was her ice cream and her syrup. "Number one, you need a flat changed. For my part, I need a certain amount of exercise every day, and I'm pretty sure tire changing qualifies.''

It might if he could figure out how to do it. One of the drawbacks of having a large staff was that there were too many things he'd never learned to do for himself.

"That's it? You change my tire and we're even?'' She looked calmer already. Evidently, rocky road worked something like Prozac.

"Uh—there's more. Now, we both know a woman in your condition shouldn't be doing a lot of heavy lifting. Those cartons might not be all that heavy, but they're bulky. You could fall, and being here by yourself, that would be dangerous.''

"So if I let you give me some money—your earnest money, as you call it—I can hire somebody to pack my stuff and load it into my car and—''

"Not exactly. What I had in mind was more on the lines of a trade. I'm paying for a room about the size of your coat closet, with a bed that's been around since the Crimean War. With no kitchen facilities, I have to take what's available in your local dining establishments, and while it's tasty, it's not exactly what the doctor ordered.''

"You're on a diet?'' She let her gaze roam at will, down, then up, then back down again. There was nothing at all sexual about it. All the same, he was uncomfortably aware of his masculinity and surprisingly aware of her femininity.

"Cholesterol's a bit high, that's all,'' he admitted gruffly.

It was really none of her business. No man wanted to admit to his physical shortcomings.

"And you want to share my kitchen?''

Go ahead, take the bait, lady. Once I get my foot in the door, I'm in like Flynn. "You'd be doing me a big favor. The doctor says all I need is a stress-free regimen of exercise and healthy foods, and I'll be back in shape in no time.''

She was nibbling. He could tell by the frown on her face. If she'd been going to shut him out, she wouldn't have waited.

He topped off his offer. "I can do your heavy lifting for you. No point in having to hire someone else.''

"How long would you want to stay?''

"We don't have to decide that right now. Anytime you want me to leave, all you have to do is ask.''

"You're not going to insist on going through with the sale?''

"Not until you're ready.''

"What if I'm never ready?''

He shrugged. "Then you stay and I go.''

The phone rang. Outside, the sounds of an outraged duck arose. Cleo struggled to rise, and Harrison handed her the phone. ''You get the phone, I'll take care of your duck.''

Four

The call was from Tally Randolf, longtime friend, one-time college roommate and, until recently, employer. Tally owned the gallery in Chesapeake where Cleo had worked as bookkeeper, show hanger, salesperson, artist liaison and anything else she could do to earn her keep.

"Hi, how ya doing, babe?" Hearing the familiar breezy greeting, Cleo sagged in relief.

"Oh, Tal—I meant to call you, but…"

"I know, I know, your line's been out of order. I tried to call earlier but nobody answered. I thought maybe you'd already sold the place and moved on."

"Mice chewed through some wires."

"Treat yourself to a few traps. Clee, why I called was, there was this guy who came in the other day looking for you. He said it was personal, but I figured that under the circumstances, you wouldn't have any personal business with a lawyer from Barnes, Barnes, whatsit and Barnes, even if he was a certified hunk. He gave me his card and said to call him as soon as you get back from vacation. I told him you'd mentioned the Virgin Islands."

"Tally, you didn't."

"Would I lie? I distinctly remember you mentioning you spent your honeymoon on Saint Croix. A mention is a mention."

"Did he say what he wanted with me?"

"Nope. I offered to let him tell me all about it over dinner, but I guess he likes skinny blondes better than Rubenesque redheads. Not that you're all that skinny these days. Hey, you think it might be trouble?"

Cleo swallowed a sudden surge of heartburn, glanced to see that her unwelcome visitor was still out of range and said, "I doubt it. He was probably in town on business and just decided to look me up before he went back to Richmond. I know who he is."

"Lucky you."

Or not so lucky. Pierce Holmes was the fair-haired boy at Barnes, Barnes, Wardell and Barnes. He'd been bootlicking his way to a junior partnership long before Niles had been killed.

"I've got his number. You want me to call him and tell him you've taken a job as lighthouse keeper somewhere in the Caribbean and can't be reached?"

"Lovely idea. D'you know of any good open-ings?"

They both knew she wouldn't be returning to her old job. She could barely support herself, much less a baby, on what Tally could afford to pay her. Tally had been the one she'd turned to when she'd had to leave Richmond. Friends since their college room-mate days, Cleo had told her everything. Tally had offered her bed, board and a job. Swallowing her pride, she'd taken all three. In today's job market, there wasn't much demand for women with three-fourths of a degree in art and no work experience.

The job was a hodgepodge, but somewhat to her surprise, she'd turned out to be good at finagling free publicity and a whiz at hanging exhibits so that each work showed to an advantage, which was an art in itself. During the five and a half years she'd been married to Niles, she'd almost forgotten she'd ever been good at anything.

"Hon? You all right?"

Cleo shook off a slew of bad memories. "Sure, I'm fine."

"Look, if you need me, I can shut up shop and be there in a few hours."

"Tal, I'm fine, honestly. But thanks. Thanks for everything."

"Well, you know me. Randolf the Ready, at your service."

"I know. She keeps on going and going and going."

Another few seconds of silence, then Tally said, "You can do it, babe. Haven't I always said you're tough as old boots? Now, repeat after me 'I, Cleopatra Larkin Barnes, am one tough broad, and I can handle anything that comes my way without even breaking a fingernail.'"

Closer to tears than laughter, Cleo dutifully repeated the familiar mantra, promised to keep in close touch and replaced the phone.

To Harrison's relief, the duck handled the threat all by herself. Before he even located her nest, he saw a nondescript snake slither into the pond and glide across to the other side. At the same moment, something small and brown whizzed past his left ear. A tiny bird, obviously startled by his presence, had ejected itself from a faded and misshapen hunting cap someone had hung on one prong of a rack of antlers.

Bird watching and snake watching. How was he going to handle all the excitement?

Allowing Cleo a few minutes of privacy with her phone call, he surveyed the surrounding woods, which were neither magnificent nor particularly exotic. He'd seen more impressive trees in Central Park. Still, there was something oddly satisfying about the collection of pines, cypresses and nondescript hardwoods.

Could it be hereditary? His roots were supposed to be here somewhere. The particular tract of land in which he'd inherited an interest was a few miles farther west. Even so, this might be considered his ancestral stomping grounds. According to the old surveyor, there'd been Lawlesses behind every third tree not too many generations back.

Not that he put much stock in such matters. He'd simply happened across a place that was attractive, available and far enough off the beaten track to make his mandatory retirement easier to manage. His decision had nothing to do with genealogy. It had still less to do with the woman.

Sure, she was needy as hell, but she wasn't his problem. Nor had he ever been burdened with an obsessive need to be needed. Until a few months ago, thousands of men and women had depended on him, either directly or indirectly. And while he modestly accepted the fact that he was a major creator of jobs and a producer of a healthy portion of the GNP, not a one of his business decisions had been influenced by a burning need to be needed.

Except for the handful who had worked for him personally—his secretaries, his chauffeur, his chef, his housekeeper and three personal assistants—the thousands of people who'd once worked for him probably hadn't even noticed when the signature on their paycheck changed.

So much for the massive ego of the so-called pirate prince.

Cleo was still sitting right where he'd left her when he stepped back into the room. Uh-oh. She had that look again.

"What's wrong?" No reaction. He'd seen the same look on the faces of an old couple in the hospital waiting room. "Cleo? Who was on the phone?"

She blinked and came back from wherever she'd been. "What? Oh, the phone. It was a—a wrong number."

Yeah. Right. And he was the queen of England.

It was none of his business, he reminded himself as he collected her bowl and his mug. "Your duck and her eggs are fine, in case you're still interested. You were right, it was a snake. Ugly devil. She handled it without my help. Are all expectant mamas so self-sufficient?"

"Mmm-hmm."

"Looked to me like a python, about sixteen feet long."

"Mmm-hmm."

"A purple python. Probably a local subspecies." He waited. And waited some more. "Look, I just had a brilliant idea. Why don't we drive into town? You get dressed and I'll change your tire, and we can drop off the flat to be repaired while we're there.''

"Mmm-hmm.''

She was no ball of fire at the best of times, but this was something else. Harrison told himself it wasn't irritation he was feeling, it was concern, and realized somewhat to his surprise that it was true. "Cleo? Listen to me. If you've got a problem, I'm a pretty good troubleshooter. Try me.''

He didn't know if he was or not. Up until recently he'd had a well-trained team of troubleshooters ready to leave at a moment's notice for any spot on the globe where there was even a potential threat to the interests of Lawless Inc.

She took a deep breath and then flashed him a smile that was obviously meant to be reassuring.

He was not reassured. Just the opposite, in fact. "Cleo? What's up?''

"Nothing's up. Stop worrying, I'm fine, but thanks, anyway.''

He studied her for a moment longer, waiting to be convinced.

The smile stretched wider. She was trying too hard. "I'll just go change into something presentable,'' she said, sounding as chirpy as that small brown bird nesting out on her back deck.

He'd spooked the bird. Someone else had done the job on her.

By the time she finished changing into her coolest maternity dress and her oldest pair of sandals, did something neat, but probably temporary, to her hair, Cleo had her emotions under control again. "You can handle it,'' she muttered, erasing the glow from her nose with powder that would disappear within minutes. "You're tough as old boots, remember?"

When it came to tearing down self-esteem, Niles had been an expert. Along with his charm and good looks, he'd inherited his father's ruthlessness, his mother's snobbishness and a sly brand of meanness that was all his own. It was a wicked combination, one that could lie dormant for months at a time, then spring forth with terrible consequences at the least provocation.

The Barneses knew about her job in Chesapeake, not that they had even pretended to care what happened to her or where she went. They probably knew she'd be selling the lodge—Henry had been furious about losing it, trying to claim it for the firm, but by then she'd had her own lawyer.

There was no way they could have found out about the baby. She'd been too careful. She'd even gone to a drugstore across town to buy the test kit. Three of them, just to be sure. Shortly after the funeral, when all three had confirmed her suspicions, she had quietly set about making plans.

Still in deep mourning for their only son, neither of her in-laws had pretended to want her to stay. They still blamed her for tricking their boy into marriage—not that she had—and for leaving him less than two years later. That, she couldn't deny. They'd even blamed her for coming back to try to patch things up.

Not that it had done any good. Niles had refused to seek help. He'd been more abusive than ever when he was drinking, and by that time, he'd rarely been entirely sober.

Cleo tried not to think about it now, because she was carrying his baby. Perhaps if she'd realized in time that she was pregnant, it might have made a difference.

Then again, perhaps not. Nothing she could do had pleased Niles. He blamed her for his drinking. Blamed her for the fact that he'd botched one case after another, until even his own father didn't trust him.

She had left him for the second time after a terrible fight late one Sunday night. Niles knew where she would go, because she'd gone there before. A cheap motel just off 250. He'd come after her. Drunk as a lord, he had sideswiped a row of parked cars and plowed down a security light before crashing through a storefront.

All her fault, of course. Not that either Henry or Vesper Barnes had come right out and said as much. It wasn't necessary. They blamed her for stealing Niles away from the woman they'd planned for him to marry.

They accused her of driving him to drink, of not staying with him when he'd needed her and of not having the decency to give him a divorce when he'd begged her for one.

She hadn't even bothered to correct them. Niles had begged her for only two things during their relationship. He'd begged her to marry him when his mother was hounding him to marry the daughter of one of her blue-blooded friends. Like a romantic fool, she'd believed him when he said he loved her.

Later—much later—he had begged her to come back to him, promising never again to touch a drop of alcohol. And she'd believed him all over again, even though by then she knew he'd been an alcoholic ever since his university days, maybe even before that. She'd believed him partly because he could be so very persuasive, but mostly because she couldn't bear to think she'd been so wrong about him in the first place.

But she had. And his parents had to have known what was going on right under their own roof. They couldn't have failed to hear all those late-night fights. The house was large, but it wasn't that large. More than once they'd seen her come down to breakfast with bruises on her face and arms. They'd pretended to believe her when she told them she'd run into a closet door or stumbled against a dresser.

If Niles hadn't been killed, she didn't know how it would all have turned out. Maybe the baby would've changed him. She would never know.

Cleo still had a scar from the first time he'd struck her, but it was the internal wounds that had come closest to destroying her—that had nearly robbed her of her self-respect, her confidence as a woman.

"It's over, let it go," she whispered. She took a moment to organize her thoughts, something she'd been doing altogether too little of lately. She'd forgotten how to think, for heaven's sake. It was so much easier just to let her mind drift along like cloud shadows out on the river, believing that once she heard from a few of her job inquiries she'd have plenty of time to choose, finish packing and leave.

Taking a deep breath, she gave her image in the mirror a critical review. "You can do whatever you have to do, Cleo Barnes. You did it for your father, you did it for yourself—now you'll do whatever you have to do for your baby. Chin up, friend, you're tough as old boots!''

Collecting her shoulder bag, keys and sunglasses, she stepped outside. ''I'm ready,'' she called from the front deck. ''Do you need to come inside and wash your hands before we go?''

Mercy, he looked as if he needed more than a hand wash. Her car was jacked up like a dog at a fireplug, the wheel hanging by a single lug. Every tool she possessed and dozens more were scattered around over the ground.

''Almost done,'' he called back, wiping his dripping brow with a greasy forearm.

She was already beginning to wilt under the direct blast of a late May sun. Harrison looked as if he'd not only wilted and melted but had been rolled in the mud for good measure.

She took the three steps down from the deck, carefully holding on to the railing. ''It might be rusty. The wheel, I mean. I've noticed signs of rust around the door frames. Around here, that usually means either salt water or fertilizer.''

He shot her a baffled look.

''What I mean is, they'll both cause rust, but people don't usually haul fertilizer in sedans, so I think mine must have been a storm victim. I bought it a few months after that big hurricane last fall, and then later, I saw this piece on TV about the dangers of buying secondhand cars in the Tidewater area after a bad storm.''

''Right. Sure. Makes sense.'' Regarding her as if he expected smoke to start coming from her ears any moment now, he pulled a filthy handkerchief from his pocket, glanced at it and put it back. "I guess I'd better finish up here before I clean up."

From the shade of a lacy cypress, Cleo watched him frown at her tire tool as if he'd never seen one before. Under several streaks of grease and a liberal coat of sweat, his face was flushed.

Heatstroke? Apoplexy? He'd mentioned his cholesterol level, but what if he was hypertensive? He seemed the type. Uptight. Inflexible. Tense. He probably shouldn't be exerting himself in the hottest part of the day.

"I've got a better idea," she said as he bent over to tackle the stubborn lug again. Standing several feet behind him, she admired the flawless cut of his khakis, and then admired the flawless cut of his rear end.

Woman, you are out of your ever loving mind! The shape you're in—the situation you're in—the last thing you need to be thinking about is a man's behind!

All the same, if the G-stringed male models in her first life class at VCU had looked anything like Harrison Lawless, she'd probably have flunked the course.

He fit the lug wrench over the nut and gave it a few hard twists. Nothing happened. Not because he lacked strength, but because the thing was obviously rusted in place.

He cursed and then apologized, which she thought was rather sweet. "Cleo?"

"What?"

"You were saying?"

"I was?"

He shot her a grin that expressed both exasperation and amusement. "I'm pretty sure one of us was saying something. Look, can this job wait until the sun goes down? I've got a perfectly good vehicle with four good tires."

She took pity on him. Sweat was already making her scalp itch and dripping down her neck. What in the world would she do if he had a heatstroke? Call 911?

She didn't even know if they had a 911 this far out in the country. Great. *Now* she worried about it. What if she'd gone into labor out here alone, with a flat tire and a dead phone?

"Fine. You go wash up and I'll make iced tea to go. You're not one of those people who frown on eating or drinking in cars, are you? My mother-in-law said it wasn't done, which is silly, because people do it all the time."

"Iced tea sounds great," said Harrison. He watched as a worried look came over her face, and waited for whatever non sequitur came next. One usually did. Forking back his hair, he wiped the sweat from his eyes with a greasy handkerchief and thought about the bar in the back of his limo. Before he'd left New York he had given Nick, the retired wrestler who'd been his driver for nine years, the keys and the title, along with a year's salary as bonus.

He'd give five thousand dollars right now to hear the ex-fighter say, "Here, man, gimme that thing before you tear up a fine piece of machinery."

Not that her car was a fine piece of machinery. It was a piece of crap. If she wasn't broke, she wasn't far from it. Why else would anyone drive a clunker like this? Why else would she put a house she obviously didn't want to sell on the market at a price that guaranteed a quick sale?

There were still a few questions he'd like answered. Not that the answers were any of his business, but with too much time on his hands, he might just make it his business. A man had to do *something,* he told himself, until he learned how to do nothing.

It hadn't sounded all that difficult, cutting back on work, learning to relax, how to enjoy life. The trouble was, he'd enjoyed just what he was doing. The hard-driving, cut-and-thrust world of big business. Seeing opportunities before his competitors did, making opportunities where none existed. Winning every race he entered, not for the money but because he'd never learned how to be a loser.

Cutting back wasn't an option. It was like telling an alcoholic he could drink in moderation. An invitation to disaster.

"And maybe peanuts," she finally said, thoughtfully. "The unsalted kind."

Yes, ma'am, one non sequitur, right on schedule.

Once they hit Highway 64, the drive into Columbia didn't take long. With the air conditioner going full blast, the woman beside him silent and no traffic to speak of, Harrison pulled up his mental file and scanned the list of things to accomplish.

The fact that she had trouble getting in and out of the high chassis turned out to be an advantage. He left her in the car with the AC going full blast and a CD playing Sibelius while he checked out of the motel. Not that she'd offered to help him pack.

"Next stop, garage. I'll just be a minute, do you mind?"

She shook her head and gave him a sleepy smile, and he wondered how a woman who was all that pregnant could look all that appealing. Not sexy— something far more feminine than that.

File and forget, Lawless. Better yet, delete the file.

He arranged for the garage to collect Cleo's car, fix the flat or replace it, give the thing a thorough inspection, repairing anything that needed it. Wherever she went from here, she was going to need a reliable set of wheels. He'd hate to see her stranded out on the highway in her condition.

A few minutes later they pulled into the parking lot of the town's only supermarket. "Want to go in with me? I might need some supervision here."

She was sucking on a milk shake. He'd never known a woman to have such a love affair with ice cream in all its various forms. "I probably could use the exercise, if I can get out of this thing without a parachute."

Grinning, he came around and opened her door, and she braced her hands on his shoulders and then gave up and let him lift her down. Harrison told himself it was the heat that made his body react the way it did, not the feel of her moist, silky skin, her soap-and-talcum scent or the sharp little gasp she uttered when her belly pushed against his.

It wasn't the first time he'd noticed it lately—this latent streak of tenderness that affected him at odd times. He hoped to hell it wasn't a symptom of anything serious.

There were fewer than a dozen customers inside.

Mostly women. A few men. Every single one seemed to know exactly what they were doing. Harrison had never been in a food store in his life.

Talk about survival skills.

He insisted on pushing the cart, not because he knew a damned thing about supermarket protocol, but because it seemed the gentlemanly thing to do. Cleo plucked things off the shelf and dropped them in. Ice cream for her, fresh fruit and vegetables for him. A package of frozen boneless, skinless chicken breasts.

In other words, a lot of raw material that he hadn't a clue how to prepare.

She picked up a carton of fresh crabmeat from an ice-filled washtub. "You like crab cakes?" she asked, peering at the price.

"My chef used to, that is, there's this thing with crab and noodles and cream and—"

"Alfredo. You probably shouldn't if you have a cholesterol problem."

They bought more chicken, this one already cooked, and a few more vegetables.

"Hedonist," he taunted when she went back for another gallon of triple-chocolate frozen yogurt.

"My cholesterol's one-sixty-three, what's yours?" she inquired innocently when he picked up a package of filet mignon, gazed at it longingly and regretfully replaced it in the cooler.

By the time they rolled up to the checkout counter they were joking like old acquaintances. They hit a slight snag when she dug out her billfold. Harrison shoved it back into her bag, telling her they'd settle up later, over drinks. "Ice-cream soda for you, black coffee for me." He'd bought the beans and ground it himself. Another first. It was half decaf, half high-test. He'd already discovered the downside of cutting out caffeine cold turkey. Headaches that wouldn't quit.

Next stop, a hardware store, not because they needed any hardware, but for the simple reason that he'd never been inside one, and he was fascinated. He was beginning to realize there was a whole world out here he'd never even bothered to explore.

Cleo teased him about being a kid in a toy shop and reminded him that her ice cream and his chicken breasts were melting. He was studying a display of salt licks.

"The last thing either one of us needs is salt. Besides, those are for cows."

"Yellow salt?"

"I think there're some minerals in it, too. I'm no expert, either."

He couldn't leave empty-handed, so he contented himself with buying a low step stool to help her in and out of the Rover.

Predictably, she protested.

Predictably, he insisted. "Would you rather I lifted you up bodily and put you on the seat every time? I don't mind." He'd never met a woman who resisted a man's help more than Cleo Barnes. Or one who needed it more.

"I'd rather be driving my own car. At least it's built for normal people."

"Are you insinuating that you're normal?"

She shot him a look that started out scathing, but he caught the quiver at the corner of her mouth. It was a nice mouth. One made for smiling. Funny thing—he had a hunch she hadn't been doing too much of that lately.

Come to think of it, neither had he.

"I don't suppose I could interest you in barbecue before we head back to the ranch, could I?" He shot her a leering look.

"I have only two words to say to that. Saturated fat."

"What, pigs are saturated?"

"To the gills. Look, Harrison, if you're going to be staying with me for a few days, maybe you'd better give me your diet list. I don't think mine would do you much good."

A few days? Think again, lady. One of us is staying permanently. And I don't plan on leaving anytime soon.

But then he caught that worried look on her face and deliberately set himself out to be charming, entertaining and distracting. It was a social skill he'd learned so long ago it came as second nature. By the time they turned off 64 onto the dusty two-lane road that led to the one-lane road that led to the lodge, they were both laughing.

It felt good. *He* felt good. A hell of a lot better than he'd ever felt working some boring social event with a glass in his hand and a phony smile on his face.

Cleo gave him his choice of rooms. Hers was the master suite, which took up the entire north wing. Each of the other two wings contained two bedrooms and a shared bath. Harrison chose a western exposure, facing the woods. The room was airy, light, not overtly feminine, but neither was it self-consciously masculine. The dark logs and paneling had been washed with a thin coat of white, and there wasn't a single trophy to be seen.

He liked it. Not that he was any expert on interior decorating. If any of his properties needed attention, he hired the best talent available and offered a minimum of guidance, insisting only on comfort, quality and no jarring colors.

This room qualified on all three counts.

Light, clean and unobtrusive. Solid pine furniture. White cotton curtains, white cotton rugs. The bed was only a queen-size, but it would do until he could have his own bed shipped down.

It was the artwork that held his eye. Art was something else he could take or leave, yet there was something about these works that held his attention. They seemed personal. Almost intimate. One was of a woman reading, her face in shadow, the details merely suggested. There was a lot of white paper showing, and some pencil lines that seemed to hint at more just out of range of the viewer.

He liked it. Damned if he didn't like all the works. The watercolors were more or less in the same style, obviously done by the same artist. Impressionistic landscapes, riverscapes, some with figures, some without, but all with the same hint of mystery, of lightness—of something just out of range of the viewer.

Harrison knew as much about art as he did about interior decoration, but he'd attended enough openings—usually under social duress—to suspect that these hadn't carried a large price tag. Yet oddly enough, they appealed to him far more than any of the expensive, showy works in his other properties.

He glanced at the signature, a tiny, penciled squiggle half-hidden under the mat. Not that he'd have recognized it, anyway. All the same, he made a mental note to ask if he could buy all five pieces along with whatever other furnishings she cared to leave behind.

Naturally, he would pay extra. Whatever she asked, which probably wouldn't be enough.

Cleo had gnawed one set of fingernails down to the quick and started in on the other by the time Harrison showed up in the kitchen. Wearing fresh khakis and a collarless shirt, glints of silver barely visible in his shower-damp black hair, he made her feel dowdy and dumpy, even though her gauzy floral tent dress, purchased on sale, had been billed as resort wear.

He'd picked up a layer of tan today, making his eyes look bluer than ever. She told herself that there was something reassuring about steady blue-gray eyes and a square jaw.

Or maybe it was just that she so badly needed reassurance.

"Nice," he said, nodding at her dress. At least she hoped it was her dress.

Or maybe she didn't.

Woman, you have lost it. Flat-out lost *it! Now, behave yourself and get serious while you still have a window of opportunity.*

"You're awfully quiet," Harrison noted. "Thinking?"

She shook her head. "Just gestating. It takes a lot

of patience. I dished up the chicken and made us a salad.''

''I was going to do that.''

The look she gave him might have shaken the self-confidence of a lesser man. ''I'll do it tomorrow,'' he conceded. ''By the way, after dinner you'd better make out a list of numbers and names and leave it by the phone, just in case.''

''In case of what?''

''In case of…well, you know. The baby.''

''Plenty of time. Sit down. I'm starving, aren't you?''

He eyed the skimpy meal set out on the table, trying to look interested. His chef would have walked out in disgust.

''Harrison, did you ever have trouble focusing?'' she asked after he'd cautiously sampled the salad, which was dressed with some thin watery stuff instead of the thick blue cheese dressing he preferred.

''Can't say that I have.''

''I think it must be something to do with hormones. Nobody told me I was going to have to prop my eyes open with toothpicks to stay awake, or that I couldn't eat cucumbers, melons or radishes, or that I'd cry over nothing and practically take up residence in the bathroom.''

''Do you?''

''Do I what?''

''All of the above.''

She nodded and then dredged up a deep sigh. ''Could I ask you a personal question? What do you do when the questions you ask don't have any answers?''

"No answers at all, or just none you want to hear?"

"I'm not sure. I guess that's one of the questions that don't have an answer."

"Oh, I suspect it does, only you're not ready to hear it."

She made a face at him, and he had to stop himself from reaching across the table and smoothing out the faint pucker between her eyebrows with his thumb. Which was odd, because he'd never been prone to physical gestures.

Harrison studied the top of her head as she toyed with her salad. The last rays of a setting sun spilled in through the window, highlighting shades of copper and bronze among the tarnished gold of her hair. Her lashes, surprisingly dark for a blonde, cast shadows on her cheeks. He found himself wondering all sorts of things about this woman who had so unexpectedly stepped into his life.

Or he into hers. The results were the same. As if he didn't have enough on his mind, he had to take on a pregnant woman with no husband and no visible means of support.

"Here's a question you can answer. How far away is your obstetrician?"

She glanced up and he watched as she pulled herself back from wherever she'd been. Brown eyes on a blonde—especially clear, pale brown eyes—were strikingly attractive. "As the crow flies? Maybe a hundred miles, give or take. Longer if you go by road. Why?"

Shaking his head, he swore softly. "I knew I

should never have driven down this road, much less stopped to read the sign. Much less come inside.''

The look she sent him was totally guileless. ''It's not too late to leave. I can give back any money you put down, so there's nothing to keep you here.''

''That's where you're wrong. Walking away might have been possible yesterday. Today it's not even an option.''

He didn't know what the hell had prompted the statement, he only knew it was true. Without knowing why, he knew he could no more leave now than he could skip over the past year and go back to where he'd been before his entire world had suddenly converged into an endless ordeal of pain.

Five

Lying in bed that night, Harrison gazed unseeingly at the impressionistic riverscape on the wall as his mind roved over his past, his present, and struggled to come to terms with the future. He missed being in the thick of things. Probably always would. The subtle excitement. The feeling of power. It was an addiction.

He'd be the first to admit that most of the glitter had worn thin as far as his social life was concerned. The playground might vary, but the players were much the same. He knew, without really wanting to know, who was sleeping with whom, who was about to declare bankruptcy, who was selling out to whom. That was one part of his old life he wouldn't miss.

But the rest—the building, the achieving—that never grew old. It was what he did. What he'd always done. All the years of seeing his ideas turned into reality...of giving the best of himself, expecting the best from others and usually getting it...of being respected by his peers, even those who hated his guts, and sought after by some of the world's most beautiful women...

Sure, he'd miss it.

But he could handle it. Considering the alternative, he would damned well have to. His cardiologist had compared his old life-style to being constantly at battle stations. He'd been so addicted to adrenaline that even in purely social situations he was on edge, never quite able to relax and enjoy where he was for looking forward to where he was headed.

More than one woman had accused him of being an impatient lover. In too much of a hurry to get on to the main course to enjoy the appetizers. But then, the women whose favors he enjoyed seldom had much to offer besides their elegant, pampered bodies. If he'd thought about it, he might have concluded they were far more interested in having those pampered bodies sufficiently appreciated than they were in having sex.

Actually, until quite recently, he'd never spent much time thinking about women as individuals. For the most part he'd divided them into three groups. The ones he slept with, the ones he did business with—more than half his immediate staff was female—and the wives of his male associates.

So what had changed? Could his brain have been affected by what had happened to his heart?

Even unpregnant, Cleo Barnes would never come close to being his type. While not always strictly beautiful, the women whose company he enjoyed most were invariably either brainy, shrewd and sophisticated, or polished, amusing and elegant.

Cleo Barnes was about as polished as a pinecone.

Yet he couldn't deny that there was a glowing quality about her he'd never noticed in any other woman. Whatever it was, he was beginning to realize it was more than skin-deep. The remarkable thing was, he liked being with her. He was comfortable around her, which was damned peculiar, since often as not she was chewing him out.

He had a feeling she wasn't too impressed with him. Women usually were. Maybe it was the novelty that appealed to him.

Or maybe not.

He forced a yawn, hoping the power of suggestion would send him over the edge. No such luck. He was like the AVUS Quattro a car-collecting friend owned. Five hundred horsepower, V-12 engine, permanently up on blocks.

"Va-room, va-room," he uttered softly.

She was afraid of something.

Or of someone.

Harrison told himself he was being overimaginative simply because he had nothing better to occupy his mind. That wasn't even the worst of it. He felt like a pervert for admitting it, even to himself, but that slow, sleepy sexuality of hers was beginning to fascinate him.

Amen and good night, Lawless. What you need is a shrink, not a cardiologist.

The birds were raising hell outside. Had he actually thought it was quiet out here in the country?

Harrison had spent another restless night. The bed was too small and not his own, but then, he seldom slept well in any of his own beds, either. Unless he dulled the edge with alcohol, which he did only on rare occasions—or exhausted himself with a woman, which he also did only occasionally.

Mostly, he lay awake thinking of new ventures and new ideas and how to put them into motion. Some people counted sheep—he went over profit-and-loss statements in his head.

When the woodpecker started hammering, he got up and showered, quietly put on a pot of coffee to brew, after guessing at the measurements, and went outside to collect the tools he'd left scattered around the day before.

The tow truck arrived shortly after he'd separated his tools from hers and replaced his in the Rover. He didn't even know the names of most of them, much less how to use them. He talked to the driver, who obviously did, about cars and about kids these days, and about what was going on in Washington, the gist of which seemed to be a pox on both their houses. The fellow was a font of wisdom.

Harrison made a few more adjustments in his opinion of life in the slow lane.

Her car was just disappearing around a bend in the road when Cleo wandered out onto the deck, drying her hair, wearing another of her shapeless tents, this one yellow with big, splashy white daisies. Barefoot, she made her way cautiously down the steps, looking freshly scrubbed and delicate despite her ungainly figure. "What's going on?"

"Just putting away the tools I left out yesterday. Ready for breakfast? I made coffee."

"Harrison, where's my car going?"

She was frowning. Not a good sign.

"You might say it's going in for a physical. I made arrangements yesterday to have it picked up."

"I had it inspected in March. It's not due for another inspection yet."

"Yeah, well, turns out your spare was bald, and what with the rust, I thought—"

"You have no right to think anything about my car."

"Cleo, be reasonable. As long as you're still here, you need dependable transportation."

"As long as I'm still here? What do you mean, as long as I'm still here?"

"Look, I probably should have mentioned it to you first. If I'd known you were going to object, I'd have told you about it, but—"

"Object! *Object?* You hijack my car, and you expect me to sit back and meekly accept it?"

"If it's a question of money, I owe you the first week's rent. That should cover it."

"I want you out of here." Her eyes were glistening with unshed tears. He didn't know whether to take her in his arms and offer comfort or clear out before she blew. "I've changed my mind about letting you stay."

"Now, Cleo, we've been over all that. The contract you signed, remember? And the offer to purchase I signed with the agency, agreeing to all your stipulations? You don't want to get all upset. It's not good for the baby."

"I am not upset! Stop patronizing me!"

Her eyes were too bright. Her chin was trembling. The tip of her nose was white, and her cheeks were flushed.

The shrill of the telephone cut through the twitter of birds and the soft swish of the river washing against the shore. They stood there for a full thirty seconds, glaring at each other. At least, Cleo glared.

Harrison, doing his best to summon up all the negotiating skills he had honed to a fine edge over the years, was his normal reasonable, tactful, patient self.

"Don't you want to answer your phone?"

"No, I don't want to answer my phone. What I want is my car back."

"It might be important," he suggested in a placating tone.

"I'm not expecting any important calls."

"Sometimes nice things happen when you least expect them."

"Did you make that up, or is it something you read on a bumper sticker?"

"I'm trying to keep in mind your delicate condition, but you're not making it easy for me." His patience slipped a notch. She was hard as hell to reason with—he'd noticed that before.

Her chin quivered. A tear spilled over.

"You're going to cry again, aren't you?"

"I am not going to cry. Stop looking at me like that."

The phone rang several more times and cut off abruptly, the ensuing silence deafening.

"How do you want me to look at you?" he asked, a quizzical smile tugging at the corner of his mouth.

"From a distance. Over your shoulder. In your rearview mirror. On your way out."

"I think you need a dose of ice cream."

"And I think you need to call the garage and tell them to bring back my car."

"Yes, ma'am. First thing after breakfast."

Clutching her belly, she turned and stalked away, bare heels digging into the carpet of pine straw and cypress needles. He watched her go, wondering how a woman could manage to look so militant and so feminine at the same time.

She was steamed. Royally steamed.

He dumped her tools in a deck chair for the time being and followed her inside, a gleam of anticipation in his eyes as he thought about the negotiations ahead.

"Yuk! What is this supposed to be, roofing compound?" She glared at him across the hatch-cover table in the kitchen, obviously not at all placated by the big bowl of cereal-covered ice cream he'd served her. He'd even topped it off with a sprinkle of unsalted peanuts.

"You don't like my coffee?" He hadn't quite got the measurements right yet, but for a first effort he thought it was pretty good. Of course, some people preferred tinted water to real coffee.

"Now, about my car—"

"About the rent check. I was thinking five hundred a week for room and board."

She dropped her spoon. "Five *hundred?* You mean five hundred *dollars? A week?*"

"Not enough?"

"It's too much, you—you looby!"

"Looby?"

Her shoulders lifted and fell in an expressive gesture, and he couldn't help but notice how delicate they were compared to her breasts, and then he got to wondering if her breasts were larger than normal. He'd heard that at a time like this, a woman's breasts could grow a whole cup size.

"What are you looking at?"

"Your, uh, neck?"

"What's wrong with my neck." It was a challenge, not a question. She had a way of framing questions that way.

"Nothing. Nothing at all. It's a nice neck. Long, but not too long—just right, in fact." He'd lost his flipping mind. Harrison Lawless, a man who could negotiate his way through a corporate minefield without even breaking into a sweat, had flat-out lost it.

She took a deep breath, throwing into further prominence the portion of her anatomy visible above the table. The portion that he was trying his damnedest not to notice. He finished his coffee, grimaced and refilled the mug with milk.

And grimaced again. "What the devil is this stuff? Are all the cows down south anemic?"

"It's skim, and stop trying to change the subject."

"I don't drink skim. Where's the milk?"

"Where's my car?"

Easy, easy. No stress, remember? "It's getting checked out so you won't break down on your way to the hospital. You don't want your son born on a back road out in the sticks, do you?"

He could see her trying to get a grip on herself. She was doing a better job of it than he was, and he was supposed to be the expert.

"Harrison, would you please just call and tell them to bring my car back? I'll buy a new tire if I have to, but they can probably stick one of those little pluggy things in the hole, and it'll be good as new. I'd really prefer not to—"

"What's a little pluggy thing?"

Regarding him steadily, she dug her spoon into her

breakfast. "You've never changed a tire in your life, have you? Admit it. I knew all along by the way you were dressed—I knew for sure when I saw the way you had that jack rigged. It's a wonder you didn't break something."

"Now, wait just a minute there, madam. Nobody goes through life without the occasional flat tire."

"Ha!" With a smug, disbelieving look, she swallowed the whole spoonful of cereal-covered black-cherry ice cream. Suddenly, a stricken look came over her face. A look of acute pain.

"What's wrong?" He was around the table like a shot. "Cleo, what is it? What hurts?"

She moaned, her eyes closed tightly. Harrison placed a hand on her stomach. Something was wrong. Something down there felt almost as if it were moving.

It *was* moving.

The thing—her son, her baby—was getting ready to move out!

He eased around behind her, his mind racing. Call 911? No, get her into the Rover, put on the emergency flashers and head for the hospital.

The hospital. Hell, he didn't even know where the nearest hospital was. "Cleo, listen to me. No, maybe you'd better lie down first. I'll get the phone book and—"

"It's my head."

It was her head. "Oh. Right."

Her *head?*

He knelt beside her, one hand on her shoulder, the other trying to avoid touching anything vital. Anything personal. Was she too warm? Feverish?

She took his free hand and placed it on the dome lifting her smock. He stopped breathing.

"There," she whispered. "Did you feel it? She's practicing her arabesques again."

He felt it. God, he could *feel* it!

"Is it—are you—is he all right?"

She smiled at him. If the sun had risen inside her, she couldn't have been more radiant. This close, he could see the fine lines fanning out at the corners of her glowing eyes like a delicate carved design on a piece of Chinese ivory. One of her front teeth had been chipped and never repaired. Lauren Hutton, eat your heart out.

She smiled, and he forgot to breathe. A pregnant stranger. A ditsy, flaky, bad-tempered woman he'd known for less than a week.

"Look, maybe you'd better lie down for a while. I've got some phone calls to make. Later on, when you're feeling better, we can make a dry run to the nearest hospital. One of us needs to know the route in case—"

"Stop worrying, I'm fine. I've still got nearly six weeks to go. By then, who knows where I'll be? I might even decide to go back to Chesapeake."

"All the same, I think you'd better lie down."

"What I'd better do is finish my ice cream, only this time I won't take such big bites. I never could figure out how it works."

"How what works?"

"You know—ice? Ice cream? Headaches? I think she noticed, don't you?"

He didn't have a clue what she was talking about,

but that was nothing new. Just as long as she wasn't going into labor.

Cleo finished her breakfast, taking tiny bites, then swallowed her vitamin pill and a few more supplements, all under Harrison's watchful eye. He didn't know what he was watching for. All the same, he felt responsible. Not because she meant anything to him, but because it was his nature. It was one of the reasons his employees—his ex-employees—had one of the best benefit packages available, including paid family leave, health and dental care, auto club memberships, health club memberships and a fully vested retirement program.

He might be a pirate, but dammit, he was a caring pirate.

As soon as she was settled in the hammock on the back deck with a glass of iced tea and an old issue of *Art in America,* he got down to the business of renewing acquaintances and calling in a few favors. Some years ago he'd established and endowed a satellite children's clinic in an inner-city neighborhood. His name was not entirely unknown in medical circles.

By noon he'd managed to secure appointments with both an obstetrician and a cardiologist at Chowan Hospital in Edenton, about thirty miles out of Columbia on the other side of the Albemarle Sound.

Feeling invigorated by his successful negotiations, he made sandwiches. Lettuce, tomato, fat-free cheese and fat-free mayo. It was hardly worth eating, but if Cleo insisted on watching his cholesterol for him, he might as well humor her.

Actually, it was kind of nice, having someone who

wasn't being paid to do it worry about him. Back in New York he'd had three personal assistants who did everything from sending out his dry cleaning to scheduling his dental appointments to ordering morning-after flowers sent to the lady of the moment.

This was entirely different.

"Hey, you're getting too much sun." He placed the tray of sandwiches on the railing and touched her arm. The single shaft of sunshine filtering through the lacy branches had shifted until it fell across her face, turning the tips of her lashes translucent, highlighting a handful of freckles scattered across her nose.

"Cleo? Wake up, darling." *Darling? Where the devil had that come from?*

Without moving, she opened her eyes and gazed up at him. "This is nice," she murmured drowsily.

"Hammocks aren't very stable. You probably ought to stay out of them until after the baby comes."

"I'm not going to fall."

"Nobody ever intends to fall. You're, uh, that is, your sense of balance might not be—"

"You mean I'm big as a blimp and about as maneuverable."

"Yeah, well. Now that you mention it..."

He grinned. So did she. His sense of accomplishment underwent a subtle shift, from the gritty triumph he'd felt on securing quick appointments with two specialists in a strange town to something gentler, far less easy to define.

"What have you been up to?" Her voice, like her smile, was drowsy, unfocused.

"Nothing much," he said modestly. "A little bit

of networking. I made lunch. No salt, no fat, no taste.''

''I could've done it.''

''You need your rest.''

''What I need is exercise. Do you think swinging in a hammock qualifies?''

He chuckled. ''Probably in the same range as changing a tire.''

They ate tasteless sandwiches and he told her about his Scottish chef, who was sensitive about his profession. ''It's probably the reason I hired him. When the agency sent him around to be interviewed, the poor guy was so defensive. He's highly qualified, but he'd been cooking in an all-night diner in Jersey because nobody would hire a chef named MacDonald.''

''He could have called himself Pierre.''

''Not with that accent, he couldn't.''

''Was he a good cook?''

''The best. His beef Wellington is world class, and no one can beat him when it comes to oysters Alfredo. The only thing I draw the line at is haggis.''

''Harrison, what are you doing here?''

He pretended not to know what she was getting at. ''Having lunch. Getting ready to drive you to the nearest hospital to interview an obstetrician, just in case.''

''That's not what I mean, and you know it. Who *are* you?''

''A retired businessman from New York.''

''At your age?'' Her eyes widened. ''Oh my. You're not an undercover agent, are you? Or someone in the witness protection program?''

"Is that what you've been thinking?" It might explain the hint of wariness he'd noticed before.

No, it wouldn't. She'd been wary the first time she'd laid eyes on him. It seemed to come and go. Phone calls made it worse.

"Answer my question. Are you?"

"I am not, nor have I ever been, an undercover agent. Nor am I presently under any type of government protection. You watch too much television."

"No, I don't. Are you a detective? Did someone send you here to—"

"Cleo, what the devil's going on? If you really believe all that, why did you let me in? Why didn't you slam the door and call the police?"

She looked confused. Maybe a little embarrassed, but mostly confused. He wanted to hold her, comfort her, sort out her problems so they could both get on with their respective lives. "Listen to me, I don't know who you think I am, or who you're afraid of, but take my word for it, I'm as harmless as anyone you're ever likely to meet. Now...isn't it about time we leveled with each other?"

"All right, then who are you?"

"I told you who I am. You want to see my driver's license? Harrison Lancaster Lawless, six foot two, one hundred and ninety pounds, plus or minus, black hair, gray eyes, organ donor."

"That doesn't tell me anything new."

"You know the rest of it. Retired businessman, primary residence until recently, New York City. Your turn now. What are you so afraid of?"

She waited two full beats before saying, "I'm not afraid of anything."

Regarding her steadily, he said, "Take your time. I'm not going anywhere. But if you need help…"

She opened her mouth, hesitated, and then said, "I need help. Harrison, would you kindly get me out of this thing? I have to go to the bathroom again."

The appointments were for two-thirty and two-fifty, respectively. They argued over his choice of hospitals. "There's more than one hospital in the area. According to the map, there's one in Little Washington, one in Plymouth and something in—"

"I talked to your doctor in Chesapeake. The number was in your address book."

"You had no right—"

"I apologize, but as long as I'm responsible for you—"

"You might be responsible for someone else, but I assure you, you're *not* responsible for me."

"Cleo, be reasonable."

"No, you be reasonable! Just because I allow you to stay in my house until we clear up this thing about the contract or the option or whatever—just because you bought a few groceries—and by the way, I owe you for those."

She started fumbling to open her purse, and Harrison swore under his breath. "Don't cry. Just don't start crying, will you?"

"I *never* cry!" She glared at him, tears spilling over her lashes. "It's—it's this blasted air conditioner of yours. It blew dust in my eyes."

"Hey—truce, okay?" He adjusted the fan control, glanced at her to see if she needed his handkerchief and saw her eyes widen as she stared straight ahead.

Quick reflexes were all that kept him from slamming into the logging truck pulling out of a side road. But even superb reflexes weren't enough to keep him from veering off into a drainage ditch.

Six

Harrison paced the floor outside the examining room. He had already sent word to the cardiologist, canceling his appointment. The cut on his forehead, which had been the least of his worries, had been dealt with in the emergency room.

He grabbed the arm of a nurse's aide hurrying past with a covered tray. "Mrs. Barnes—is she all right? Can you find out what's going on in there?"

The woman looked at him, looked at his hand, which he promptly removed from her arm, and then seemed to relent. "I'll check again, but if she's not gone up to delivery, she's probably okay. You sit down and stop worrying, y'hear? You look worse'n she does."

He sat for all of two minutes, and then he began to pace again. While he paced, he made mental lists of things to do and things to buy on the way home.

Or maybe it would be better to take her home and come back—

No, he couldn't leave her alone until he was certain there would be no repercussions.

Flowers. He'd buy her flowers. And low-dose aspirin. That was for him. He hadn't been taking them regularly, but after giving his heart such a jolt, maybe he'd better start again.

An answering machine. She'd mentioned yesterday that she was supposed to walk every day. This way she wouldn't have to worry about missing a call. A couple of cellular phones would come in handy, too.

What else did a woman need when she was about to give birth? All he could think of was hot water. In the movies someone was always told to boil water. He had a feeling that no longer applied.

What she really needed was to move into town, where she'd be closer to the hospital. Not much chance of that. He'd settle for a few more phones. And while he was at it, he'd better take down the hammock and buy her a chaise longue for the deck. A wide one. Something with strong, steady legs. Better yet, he'd order one for each deck and have them delivered first thing tomorrow.

And he might as well stock up on ice cream.

Ice cream. Lounge chairs and ice cream? Was this the same Harrison Lawless described in *Prominence Magazine* as one of the world's most eligible *bachelors?* An international wheeler-dealer seen in all the world's plushest watering holes with some of the world's most sought-after women?

By the time the piece had come out, months after the interview, he was being described by a few hacks as the world's most elusive bachelor. Whether that was because he was skilled at eluding marriage or skilled at eluding the media, he didn't know.

Thank God there was no press around now. When word had leaked out that he'd been admitted to a hospital, his PR people had spun it into a routine insurance physical, with an added few days of therapy for a pulled muscle. Interest had died down. But once he'd started the process of liquidating his assets, the speculation had sprung up all over again. Wall Street had rumbled a couple of times before his people had managed to get a handle on it.

Now he no longer had to worry about spin control. For the most part, the media had moved on to the latest political scandal, the hottest new bachelor, the most recent Hollywood gossip. But he'd just as soon keep a low profile. If word got out that one of the world's most eligible bachelors was shopping for ice cream and deck chairs for a flaky blonde with a slow smile and a big belly, a few eyebrows might lift.

The aide helped her get dressed again. Cleo was grateful. She'd been given a clean bill of health, but she was still shaken. If it hadn't been for Harrison's quick reaction, she might've been—

She refused to think about "might've-beens."

"Think positive thoughts." She'd read that somewhere. On a maternity T-shirt? Or maybe it was Norman Vincent Peale.

Tally had said, Think pink. Tally wanted a baby girl.

Cleo didn't care what her baby was, as long as it was healthy. She eased down off the examining table, instinctively cradling her precious excess cargo in her arms. The doctor had told her not to be surprised if a few bruises showed up over the next day or so. He'd advised her to expect a certain amount of stiffness, too, because she'd clenched every muscle in her body.

But the baby was fine. Just fine. *Thank you, God.*

"Right across the hall," the aide directed her. "Dr. Jane wants to give you some pamphlets and maybe a prescription. I reckon you've already read everything there is to read about babies. Most women have by the time they get this far along, but humor her. She's only been working here a few months.''

Cleo listened dutifully to a brief lecture, accepted the pamphlets, promised to walk at least half an hour a day, preferably early mornings or late afternoons. She promised to call if there was the least indication of spotting or any unusual pain, and to come back in two weeks.

Feeling like an armored tank that had just come through a battle, partly because Dr. Jane was tall, slender and beautiful, not to mention insufferably cheerful, she waddled out of the doctor's tiny cubicle and practically barged into Harrison, who was standing there with the gray-haired aide who had helped her dress and undress.

There was a strip of adhesive on his forehead. He looked worried. He looked awful, in fact. "If I was you," the aide advised, "I'd take 'im home and put 'im out of his misery. He wore out a good pair of shoes pacing the floor.''

Harrison kept cutting worried glances at her on the way back across the bridge until she told him he was making her nervous and to please watch where he was going.

He said something about excellent peripheral vision.

She said, "Huh!" but then had the grace to add, "I don't know about that, but at least your reaction time is good. Thank you for that, Harrison.''

"Don't thank me," he said tersely. "If it weren't

for me, this wouldn't have even happened." For the past few hours he'd been fighting a load of guilt, anxiety and this crazy tenderness that was beginning to worry him.

"You're right. If it weren't for you, I'd probably have drifted along in my nice pink funk until I went into labor, and then it would be too late. My tire would still be flat, and I wouldn't know whether to bribe a taxi to drive me all the way to Chesapeake or to start looking through the yellow pages for the nearest midwife."

"You'd have handled it just fine," he assured her, but Cleo knew better. She'd really, *really* been in a funk when he'd turned up the other day. It wasn't like her. The last time she'd been like this had been the first time she'd left Niles, after he had knocked her down and then kicked her.

Actually kicked her!

Niles, with his fancy pedigree. With his degree from the University of Virginia and another one from Yale Law School. Niles, who had criticized her for the way she dressed, for the way she wore her hair, for chatting with clerks and deliverymen and treating his mother's staff as if they were family.

She might have lacked what Niles had called class, but he had lacked something far more important. When things had reached the point where she'd feared him more than she loved him, she had walked out. Not just once, but twice. By that time, she'd already reached the conclusion that in cases where there weren't any answers, it was easier not to ask questions.

"Are you comfortable? Not too warm?"

*Put it behind you. You're a survivor, remember?
Tough as old boots.* She shook her head. "I'm fine."

"How about the air conditioner? Want me to turn
it up or down?"

"No, I'm just fine, honestly. Couldn't be better.
This is really a lovely drive, isn't it? Have you ever
walked around Edenton and looked at all the old
houses? It's ancient. Dates back at least three hundred
years. They say Blackbeard had a house there." She
reached behind her to jab a hairpin back into what
had started out as a french twist.

"Does your neck hurt? Did the doctor examine you
for whiplash? It's not too late to go back."

She didn't know whether to laugh, cry or get out
and walk. At the rate he was creeping along, she'd
get there faster. "Will you please relax? From the
looks of it, you're in far worse shape than I am. What
about your head? Does it hurt? Did you have to have
stitches? Are you seeing spots before your eyes? Do
you think we'd better pull off the road and let you
rest? I'd offer to drive, but I've never driven a stick
shift. Actually, I'm not even sure I could fit under the
wheel, but I'm willing to give it a try if you're feeling
faint."

He grinned, and then he started to laugh. "Okay,
okay, you win. I'll let up if you will. Since you're in
such terrific shape, would you mind if I stopped in
town to pick up a few things?"

"Not at all. And by the way, whiplash doesn't
show up right away." He suddenly looked so concerned, she relented. "I've never experienced it personally, but my husband was a lawyer, remember?
I've heard every lawyer joke in the book."

He parked in the shade of a sprawling live oak tree and Cleo waited in the car while he went inside. With the air conditioner on low and a CD playing something weird but soothing, she forced herself to stop drifting and face up to reality.

Reality being that with no job in sight, she couldn't afford to keep the lodge even if she wanted to. She could hardly expect any employer in his right mind to hire her until after the baby was born. What on earth had she been thinking of? Tally had tried to warn her, but she'd refused to listen.

She still had a roof over her head as long as she stayed here. But her chance of finding a job in the area, even if she dared risk staying in a place where the Barneses could easily find her, was practically nonexistent. Without a job, she couldn't afford to pay property taxes, couldn't afford to buy groceries. Not to mention the fact that she couldn't afford health insurance.

Catch-22. Too many questions, no answers.

She simply hadn't bothered to think things through until Harrison had showed up, threatening to take away the very roof over her head. Much less think about how hard it would be to give up the closest thing to a home she had at the moment. Her last link to Niles at his best, in the early days of her marriage.

She supposed it could've been worse. What if the purchaser had been one of those cigar-chewing, hard-drinking, poker-playing jerks who called all women "little lady"? The type who would use the lodge for drunken orgies and then go out and shoot up everything in sight?

At least Harrison would never do that. He was

bossy and stubborn—couldn't even change a tire. He'd had her car towed without consulting her first because he'd been too ashamed to admit he didn't know diddly about changing tires.

But to be fair to the man, he'd thought he was doing her a favor.

He couldn't make coffee, either. He'd wasted half a loaf of bread trying to make a decent piece of toast. If he could do anything at all, she had yet to discover what it was. The truth was, he was useless.

Ornamental, oh my, yes. But utterly useless.

At least he was nonthreatening. In her present hormonal state, she was even beginning to think of him as a protector, if not a provider. He was certainly of no sexual interest, in spite of his obvious virility, she told herself as she watched him stride along the sidewalk carrying a stack of boxes and a fistful of shopping bags.

It occurred to her then that, in spite of everything, she instinctively trusted him. Which was more than she could say of most men. For too long she had believed in fairy tales and happily-ever-after endings.

But that was before reality had shattered her last few illusions.

It was a new experience, playing Santa Claus and nursemaid all rolled into one. Harrison, priding himself that he was getting pretty damned good at both roles, made Cleo slip off her sandals and lie down on the couch while he fixed lunch.

"Did you know you can buy iced tea already made?" he called out from the kitchen. "One percent. That's okay, isn't it?"

"One percent *tea?*"

"One percent milk. Still tastes like ditch water, but it's better than scum."

"Skim," she called back, and he could hear the undercurrent of laughter in her voice.

He began to hum as he put away the groceries. He'd made another run at the supermarket on the way through town. This time, an old hand, he had braved the task alone.

Nearly alone. With the help of a friendly clerk, he'd stocked up on frozen foods, packaged foods, instant this and ready-made that. Mac would have a fit if he could see him now, Harrison thought, humming the theme from *Finlandia* as he followed the instructions on a couple of frozen entrées.

It was a cinch. So was operating a microwave. He had a degree in electronics, after all. He poured the tea, which wasn't as good as hers, but it was passable.

What he'd really like to have was a Reuben sandwich and a tall, cold Dos Equis. Fat chance of either. According to the experts, wine was in, beer was out. "If fruit and vegetables are supposed to be so damned good, what's the difference between grapes and hops? Answer me that, Dr. Crackbone," he muttered, arranging things on a serving tray.

She was lying on the sofa, her eyes closed and the mound of her belly pulling her skirt halfway up over her thighs. She had nice legs. Not terribly long. She wasn't a tall woman. Exceptionally nice knees. Pretty feet, even if they were a bit swollen. Nice toenails.

Toenails? Jeez. You're breaking my heart, Lawless.

He bent over to place the tray on the coffee table, and it hit him all over again. Instant replay. He'd taken his eyes off the road for one single instant. In that one moment, the logging truck had pulled out onto the highway. Three lives could have been snuffed out. Maybe four.

Sweat filmed his forehead. He felt a slight twinge in his chest and thought, *Not now, God—please. This is* not *a good time.*

Take a deep breath. Stay calm. Inhale, hold, exhale. Do it again. And again.

Whew. Another crisis averted. "Here we go, can you sit up? Need some help?" He slid her tray closer and decided against slipping an arm behind her to ease her into a sitting position. Touching her had a peculiar effect on him. He was feeling shaky enough without any additional stress.

Stepping back, he took another deep breath, inhaling the mingled scent of talcum powder, shampoo and stale herbs. "It was billed as chicken cacciatore," he apologized. "I followed the instructions, but I'm afraid it doesn't look much like the picture on the box."

Nor did it taste even faintly like Mac's version of the dish. He wished it was better. Wished Mac was here to cook for them. Wished he'd never come here in the first place, never heard of the legacy that had brought him here, never had the heart attack, never…

But then, look at all he would have missed.

"The tea's not bad," he said encouragingly.

It wasn't good, either, but it was better than the chicken. He'd bought bagged salads and bottled dressing. They were no better than the rest of the meal. God, he missed Mac. He wondered if he could lure him away from his present employer and bring him down here to the lodge. He was going to have to hire staff pretty soon, anyway. He could make a bed, do the simple stuff, but he had an idea there was more to housekeeping than that.

They ate in silence. Harrison wondered what Cleo was thinking about, and then wondered if she was wondering what he was thinking about. He glanced up once or twice to see her watching him. She'd duck her face and pretend to be fascinated by an over-cooked noodle.

He insisted on cleaning up, which meant stashing the remains of their dinner in the raccoon-proof gar-bage container out by the pan where she fed the crows and putting their few dishes in the dishwasher.

"Where does the soap go?" he called out from the kitchen.

"What soap?"

In the end, she had to show him how to operate a dishwasher. He couldn't believe how many things there were that he didn't know how to do. Didn't know, because he'd never had to know, never even had occasion to wonder about them. Harrison Law-less, product of Exeter, of Harvard and MIT, a man who had built entire companies from the ground up. A man who was on a first-name basis with royalty on two continents.

Life was full of new experiences, he told himself. Feeling stupid was just one of many.

Later on, he brought a stack of boxes inside and opened them. The first was the answering machine. Bottom of the line. There hadn't been much choice. She asked him to record the message, giving only the phone number.

He gave her one of the two portable phones he'd bought, and after she retired for the night, he took the other one to his room.

An hour and a half later, he leaned back in the bed that was too short, too narrow, too soft, and smiled a smile that more than a few of his former adversaries would have recognized.

He'd been called a prince, a pirate and, on rare occasions, a predator. This was his predator smile.

Early the next morning, after a surprisingly restful night, Harrison woke to the sound of a ringing phone. He reached out and then reconsidered. It was still her house. He'd given the number out to several people last night, but he owed her the courtesy of allowing her to answer her calls.

It rang four times and he heard his own voice cut in with a brief message. And then he heard another voice, one he didn't recognize, saying, "Cleo, this is Pierce Holmes. I've been trying to reach you. I called several times yesterday, but either you were out or you weren't taking calls. At any rate, I need to see you, so how about returning my call at your earliest convenience. And, Cleo—this is personal. It has nothing to do with Henry, I promise you."

Henry? Who the hell was Henry?
Who the hell was Pierce Holmes?

They had breakfast together. Neither of them mentioned the earlier phone call. She'd glanced at the machine with its blinking red light when she'd passed by but hadn't bothered to retrieve the message. Which meant that either she'd already heard it, or she didn't want him to hear it.

They ate a boring, healthy breakfast. Harrison thought longingly of Mac's omelettes, with bacon, cheese, salsa, sour cream and mushrooms.

He thought about the twinge he'd experienced yesterday and the momentary breathlessness that had accompanied it. It had passed so quickly he'd barely had time to react. All the same, it was time to get back to the prescribed regimen. Low fat, low stress, regular exercise and the dozen or so servings of fruit and vegetables that were supposed to bring his cholesterol down to a relatively safe level. With medication, he'd got it down to three hundred. Which wasn't good, but it was a damned sight better than where it had been. He was shooting for two-twenty without medication, once he learned to stick to his damned diet.

With no more expression than if she'd been commenting on the weather, Cleo said, "I've decided to let you have the lodge."

Harrison choked on his coffee and grabbed another napkin. "You've what? What brought that on?"

"You can't be all that surprised. You're the one who keeps reminding me of the option you signed."

He waited, knowing she reacted to silence the way iron filings reacted to a magnet.

"Well, anyway, it's not going to happen right away. Closing takes anywhere from thirty to ninety days. There are all the inspections."

Inspections. That would be to satisfy bank requirements. He had no intention of telling her that inspections weren't necessary. That he never involved his bank in minor purchases. "Fine. Whatever you say. I'm not at all demanding."

"Ha! And I'm not at all pregnant."

He chuckled. "Point to you." Rising, he rinsed out the dishes and stacked them in the dishwasher the way she'd shown him the night before, taking pride in having to be shown something only once. And then he heard her sigh. "What? Now what am I doing wrong?"

"You don't put in dirty dishes without first unloading the clean ones."

"I knew that. I was just waiting to see if you'd notice."

They settled a few domestic issues, and then Cleo confronted him with that brass-tacks expression that made her pointy little chin look almost aggressive. "Harrison, yesterday at the hospital the nurse's aide told me that my handsome friend had decided not to see the cardiologist until later. Would you care to tell me what that was all about?"

"Your handsome friend, huh? You think she mistook me for your, uh, significant other?" His gaze moved pointedly to the most prominent portion of her anatomy.

"Oh, stop it. What I want to know is, why would you be seeing a cardiologist? Does it have something to do with your cholesterol? Just how high is it, anyway? Is there something you're not telling me?"

Cleo told herself later it was as if a door had been shut in her face. One minute they were joking about his not knowing how to operate a dishwasher, the next minute that glacier look was back.

"As a matter of fact, there are several things I

haven't told you. Go to the bathroom, then put on your walking shoes. We'll start out with half a mile in each direction, and I'll tell you what you want to know.''

''You're not going to tell me what I want to know, you're going to tell me what you want me to know, and no more.''

''You're right. Now, go get your walking shoes on.''

''My walking shoes don't fit anymore, and stop trying to boss me around.''

He glanced at her feet and then back at her face. ''Then put on your sandals. We'll take it easy.''

''Look, just forget it, all right? I don't need any answers, and I certainly don't need a keeper.''

''Are you sure about that?''

God, he was smooth. Niles at his best couldn't hold a candle to this man. She'd once heard a certain Virginia politician described as a velvet-covered steamroller.

Harrison didn't even bother with the velvet covering.

''All right, all right, I'm going,'' she snapped. She felt like crying. Felt even more like kicking something. Her emotions were all over the place these days. It was like PMS, only a hundred times worse.

She put on her sandals and went to the bathroom again. If her baby dropped any lower, she might as well take up permanent residence there.

He was waiting on the front deck, staring out at the river. He turned quickly at the sound of the door, almost as if he hadn't been expecting her. As if he'd been lost in thought. A million miles away. For just an instant she caught a look in his eyes that was so bleak she almost reached out to him.

"I'm ready," she said, her irritation of a moment before gone. Vaporized.

It occurred to her then that for all his bossiness, all his uptight, inept, maddening ways, Harrison Lawless was one of the loneliest men she'd ever had the dubious pleasure of knowing.

Seven

Neither of them spoke for several minutes. They walked as far as the place where the river cut in closest to the road. Harrison checked his pace to match hers. His every instinct was to stride out ahead, as if he could outdistance his irritation. He might have known she would pick up on his impatience.

"You go on ahead," she said, already panting. "I'm too slow."

But he wasn't off the hook yet. That much was implicit in the look she gave him. Sooner or later he was going to have to answer a few questions. He owed her that much. "I'm in no hurry," he lied. "I thought we'd both start out easy, maybe half a mile in each direction with a bathroom break in the middle."

She caught his hand and gave it a shake. "Oh, for heaven's sake, stop being so darned understanding. It makes me uncomfortable."

"Uncomfortable?"

"Yes, uncomfortable! But then, everything lately makes me uncomfortable, so don't take it personally. At least you don't give me heartburn."

He chuckled at that. Briefly. And then he concentrated on the pace. His normal walking stride was roughly thirty inches. Hers was about sixteen.

They strolled. It drove him up the wall. He was a strider by nature, not a stroller. He had too much pent-up energy to waste time meandering down country roads. After almost a week, the novelty of the slower Southern pace was beginning to wear off.

Dammit, he wasn't ready to be put out to pasture yet. To be dry-docked, at his age. He'd almost sooner shoot for the moon and die trying to reach it.

"Stop clenching your fists, Harrison. It makes the veins in the side of your neck bulge."

She was right. He could feel it. Feel the pressure building. He made a deliberate effort to relax. Breathe in, breathe out. Smell the damned roses. She stepped on a pinecone, flung out her arms, and he caught her by the shoulders. "Careful there—we don't want a calamity."

"No wonder I can't stand up, I'm shaped like a lopsided top!" She clung to his arm just long enough to catch her breath, muttered some dire threat against trees that littered, shook off his arm and waddled forth. "This is disgusting, Harrison. Pray you don't ever get pregnant. You don't have the temperament for it."

"It may come as a surprise to you, my dear, but that's not all I don't have."

She shot him a cheeky smile, and he could feel the tension begin to ebb. She was a comfortable woman. That is, she was when she wasn't chewing him out.

Or turning him on.

They were halfway back to the lodge when a delivery truck rattled past on the rutted dirt road, kicking up a cloud of dust. "Now, where on earth do you suppose he's going? There's not but one house on this road, and that's mine.''

He didn't bother to correct her as to whose house it was. They'd had that argument too many times. Harrison knew where the truck was headed. He'd ordered three deck lounges from a furniture store in Manteo that had promised quick delivery. "Why don't I run on ahead and check it out?"

"He'll be back as soon as he realizes he's taken a wrong turn, but go ahead. You're dying to run, anyway.''

His broad grin told her she was right on target. Cleo watched him round the bend, admiring his easy, long-legged stride. He wasn't a showy runner. No pumping elbows or fancy running clothes. He simply looked…good.

He looked good doing whatever he happened to be doing or trying to do, whether aligning the things on the mantel with mathematical precision or rearranging her cereal boxes in alphabetical order, from bran to Cheerios to Fruits 'n' Nuts to oatmeal—or even changing a tire.

He was an attractive man.

Correction—he was a strikingly handsome man with an aura of power and authority, even though he was a complete klutz when it came to actually doing anything useful. Efficient, he was not.

Cleo trudged along down the rutted road, shaking her left foot now and then to try to dislodge whatever it was that was sticking her in the foot.

In no particular hurry, she stopped to watch a couple of local fishermen tending crab pots. She watched a chunky yacht bristling with outriggers and pennants go past and wondered idly where it was bound. She thought about baby names again. She was up to the *R*s now, torn between Ramona and Rebecca.

Or Robert after her father if it was a boy.

Breaking off a stem of tall grass and using it to shoo away insects, she plodded on toward the lodge, thinking about Niles, feeling sad for what might have been, for what he'd ruined.

She thought about Harrison Lawless and felt—

Oh, she didn't know. Irritation? Aggravation? Admiration?

A combination of all those and more.

Back at the lodge, she hobbled over to the steps and sank down on the middle one, winded. There'd been a time not too long ago when she'd climbed up and down ladders five dozen times a day, unhanging and rehanging heavy framed paintings.

The delivery truck was still there, pulled up behind Harrison's car. Truck. Whatever the thing was. From somewhere at the back of the house, she could hear the low murmur of male voices. For the past three weeks she'd hardly seen another soul. Now all of a sudden, the place was running over with visitors. Tow trucks. Delivery vans. What next, a parade of door-to-door salesmen?

She kicked her foot, but whatever was in her sandal refused to budge. She couldn't bend over far enough to go in after it with a finger. That was a new development, too. Either she'd gained a pound in the last half hour, or something had shifted.

She took the line of least resistance, something she'd become remarkably good at lately, and settled back to catch her breath. Maybe she could apply for a job as a bridge tender. That shouldn't require too much exertion.

And maybe, if she didn't snap out of it, she'd find herself right back where she'd been before Harrison had turned up. Drifting along in a totally nonproductive fog, waiting for all those wonderful job offers to start pouring in.

Two men came around the corner of the house, Harrison and a red-faced stranger in dark green coveralls who looked as if he could use a glass of something cold to drink.

So could she. She was about to suggest it when Harrison slipped the man a bill, dismissed him with a casual nod and turned to where she was sitting. Sprawling. Graceful, she was not.

Planting his fists on his hips, he assumed a familiar king-of-all-he-surveyed attitude. "All finished with your walk?"

"I've got something in my left shoe. Besides, the road needs grading. It's too rutty to walk on. Once it rains, it'll flatten out some, but then it'll be too muddy."

"Hmm."

"What did he want? Did he have the wrong address? Why did you give him money?"

"Left shoe? Right shoe?"

"Left." He was impossible to distract, whereas she found it impossible to stay focused for more than five consecutive seconds. Two more different personalities would be hard to find.

He knelt and lifted her foot off the ground. It wouldn't go very far without toppling her backward. She braced her elbows on the top step while he dug out a broken holly leaf, dusted off the sole of her foot and slipped her sandal back on. At the touch of his fingers on her arch, heat sizzled all the way up her leg.

He studied her a minute, making her uncomfortably aware of her damp, flushed face, her rumpled smock, the hair that had started out pinned neatly on top of her head but was now sliding out from under its restraints.

She was a mess. He was far too polite to mention it, and she didn't know why she cared anyway, but she did. Maybe because her ego had taken such a beating over the past few years, she was desperate for the slightest measure of reassurance.

Only it wasn't reassurance he was offering. All he was offering was money and an impersonal sort of kindness out of consideration for her awkward situation. Which should be more than enough, only somehow, it wasn't.

"Want to walk some more, or would you rather stretch out in the shade with a tall, cool glass of tea?"

"You have to ask?"

With a grin that looked suspiciously smug, he pulled her to her feet, held her by the shoulders and turned her toward the deck.

It was then that she saw it, half-hidden by the redwood deck chairs and matching cross-legged table. The frame was yellow. The cushions, still covered in clear plastic, were a splashy red, lime and royal blue tropical print. It looked totally out of place in the muted rustic setting.

"What is that thing?"

"A hostess gift?"

"Harrison, what's going on here? Have you already started moving in?"

"You could say that."

"Yes, but—*look* at it. It doesn't even *look* like you."

"I sincerely hope not," he said dryly. "But wait till you see how it feels. It's not too low, easy to get in and out of. You couldn't tip it over if you tried. Come on, you can be the first to try it out."

He'd bought it. For her. Not for the world would she hurt his feelings, but given a choice, she'd have suggested something in redwood, with cushions in a muted earth tone or maybe a fern print.

"It's a little gaudy," he admitted, "but the manager said it was more stable than anything else he had in stock. I told him it was for a woman who was eleven months pregnant with triplets." She choked off a giggle. "Hold on while I get the plastic off." Using a monogrammed silver penknife, he ripped through the protective covering, pulled it aside and then watched as she carefully lowered herself onto the thick cushions.

"Well? What do you think?"

Cleo looked up at him and sighed. How could a man be so darned overbearing and so irresistible at the same time? He watched her like a hawk. "It's...nice. Soft."

"But not too soft. Just right, huh?"

He looked so anxious she took pity on him. "Harrison, it's perfect. It's wonderful. It might be a little, um, bright—"

"Gaudy. I expect it's more suited to a beach cottage than a log cabin in the woods, but it's sturdy.

And the back's adjustable.'' He was still towering over her, looking as if a single word of criticism would burst his balloon, so she tried one of his tricks. Distraction.

''Do you suppose I could have a glass of iced tea?''

Heaven help her, what was she going to do with the man? This whole situation was getting out of hand. The idea of paying rent on a house he was in the process of buying. Of sharing it with the former owner while they settled the details. If she let him, he'd wait on her hand and foot, and it was obvious he couldn't even take care of himself.

He was a drifter, whatever he'd been in the past. A businessman who'd lost his business? A husband who'd lost his wife? A man who'd lost his memory?

An escaped lunatic?

An escaped convict? She'd heard on the radio about some man escaping from a road gang just yesterday....

But then, Harrison had turned up before that.

Whoever and whatever he was, someone around here—she refused to name names—was definitely a candidate for the butterfly-net brigade.

There were three of the things, one for each deck, all equally colorful, all sticking out like enormous sore thumbs in the muted wooded setting.

Niles would have had a fit. He'd had the redwood deck furniture custom-built. It was exactly like furniture she'd seen for sale in practically all the better outdoor furniture places, but he'd insisted on having it built to order and paying twice as much as it was worth. Typical Niles. It was an ego thing.

Harrison had taken the hammock down and hidden it away. Darn it, she liked that hammock. It was one of her favorite spots to nap. However, knowing how hard it was for a leopard to change its spots, or for a control freak to change his bossy ways, she let it pass without comment.

Over the next few days, Cleo allowed a lot of things to pass without comment, including the plumber who came to inspect the plumbing, the electrician who came to check out the wiring. Something—squirrels or mice—had chewed through a couple of places, but other than the fact that the outside lights on the west side didn't work, it was in good condition. As for the rest, the roof didn't leak, there was no buildup in the chimney, no nests. The foundation had settled slightly—sooner or later it would need attention, but there was no immediate danger.

Still, it was a good thing she'd agreed to sell the place. She had a feeling repairing a settled foundation would cost a mint. Fortunately, Harrison didn't appear worried. Whatever his problem was, it didn't seem to be money.

Amazingly, it turned out that he had relatives in the area. Or at least, some of his ancestors had lived here at one time. Most of the workmen spent as much time chatting as they did inspecting. Harrison had encouraged it, listening to tales that sounded suspiciously tall to her, and with the meter running, no less. Still, he seemed to enjoy it, and as he'd already informed her, he was footing the bill for the inspections and any work done as a result.

It irritated her that the bigger and clumsier she grew, the mellower he seemed to become. These days he was so relaxed he grinned almost as often as he frowned. Several times she even heard him laugh.

They still argued. Sometimes she even won. It was a new experience, one that made her feel confident even though she was physically miserable, what with the heat, the heartburn and her constant trips to the bathroom.

After jeering at her for feeding crows in an old skillet in the backyard, he bought new bird feeders and put them up with no more damage than a few bruised thumbs, a few dozen bent nails and a generous supply of swearwords. They watched eagerly for the first visitors, watched the newly hatched baby ducks' first swimming lessons and commiserated with each other when Mama Mallard and her seven children left the pond and waddled down to the river.

She wouldn't have believed a man could change so much in such a short time. He was even drinking decaffeinated coffee and skim milk and fussing when they ran out of grapefruit.

Of course, he was still unbearably bossy. Once he discovered where she kept her few yard tools, he insisted on trying them all out. He whacked down the weeds around the house so that she wouldn't worry about it and try to do it herself.

She never had. Weeds were nice. Some had berries, some had flowers, some had interesting seeds. Most were lovely in the fall. She'd once done a series of weed studies in pen and ink.

But he had energy to spare and she had none at all.

It was easier to let nature—and Harrison—take its course.

He'd been there a little over two weeks. It seemed like two months. Seemed almost as if they'd lived there together for years. They'd given up even pretending that she was leaving. At this point, the only logical thing to do—and she'd known it instinctively all along—was to stay right where she was until after the baby came.

Once she was on her feet again, Harrison could micromanage her relocation the same way he did everything else. All she would have to do was give him a list of specifications—small town, preferably one with an art gallery and good schools. North or South Carolina or even Georgia. Not Virginia. Henry Barnes had too many sources of information in Virginia.

But all that could wait until later. Meanwhile, Harrison refused to let her lift a finger. He made her walk a mile a day, made her drink milk, take naps and vitamins, and hummed while he was doing it.

She couldn't stand a cheerful dictator. She hummed right back at him, only she couldn't carry a tune, and seeing him wince didn't help her case at all.

At least she refused to let him smoke his stinky old cigars, which he'd mentioned once he was trying to give up. She saw that he ate five servings of fruit and vegetables each day, took his low-dose aspirin and ran at least three miles every morning.

Actually, they took care of each other. When she thought about it, it made her feel like crying.

But then, everything these days made her feel like crying.

Equipment began to arrive. A computer, fax machines, various exercise machines. Harrison worked out while Cleo read aloud from books on nutrition and stitched baby clothes. She'd forgotten the pleasure she'd once derived from designing and sewing her own clothes. There'd been a time when she'd had a real flair for it, but that was before she'd married into a family that considered anything with flair illbred.

They listened to the news, local and network, and discussed getting a satellite dish. As if she'd be here long enough to benefit. The prisoner was still on the loose, according to the local news report. Harrison warned her to keep the doors and windows locked while he was out running.

"It's too hot, and besides, no escaped convict with half a brain would hang around here. He'll be long gone by now."

"Then I'll stay home. Who needs to run in this heat?"

"You do. Go earlier, while I'm still asleep."

"This place is far too isolated. I'll see about having the AC checked over and a security system installed."

"I thought that was what you liked about the place—its isolation and all the fresh air. You could breathe air-conditioning in New York."

"I'm not going to argue, Cleo. Just remember, until I get a security system installed, I want you to stay close."

As if she could waddle very far in her condition. She told him so, and they shared another laugh. A nice, comfortable, no-tension, stress-free chuckle.

"I'm beginning to believe you're good for me," Harrison told her.

"I'm beginning to believe you're bad for me. You make it entirely too easy to procrastinate."

"Hey, I can't take credit for that. You're a natural."

She threw a pillow at him. "Actually, you're good for me, too. You make me feel almost competent, which makes me feel more confident. I needed that."

He looked as if he'd like to ask questions, but didn't. Instead, he said, "Mutual benefit. You make me feel calm, lazy, a lot more comfortable than I ever thought I could be in the slow lane. It's a new experience."

"I'll just bet it is. You never did specify what line of business you were in. Are you sure you aren't a race-car driver? How about a jet pilot? No, I've got it—you're European royalty hiding out from the latest palace scandal." He was such fun to tease. She had a feeling he wasn't used to it, which made her even more curious about his past. "No, not that—the accent's wrong." Tilting her head, she regarded him with a slight frown. "The accent, maybe, but not the attitude."

She let him drag her out to walk twice a day, early mornings and late in the evening, after the sun went down. They were down to half a mile each time now, which was more than she wanted to do, but she did it for Agatha. Or Arrowsmith. If her parents had had a son, they'd probably have called him that, or maybe Apollo. She'd got as far as Wilhelmina and started back at the beginning.

Harrison insisted on accompanying her, although she could practically hear him gnashing his teeth at her snail's pace. He was sweet. He was also arrogant, inept, bossy, kind and generous. She was halfway to being in love with the man—another symptom of hormones in chaos—when he announced that he'd invited a friend to visit and would be meeting her at the airport in a few days.

She couldn't believe the crushing disappointment she felt at the thought of someone else—another woman—invading their private world. It had been so peaceful, so perfect with just the two of them.

"Fine. That's wonderful. There's certainly plenty of room. In fact, I've been thinking, I really should move out of the master suite and take one of the smaller guest rooms. Or maybe even look for a place closer to the hospital. Now that I think about it—"

"Cleo. Kindly shut up a minute, will you? Her name is Marla Kane and you'll like her."

"Fine. That's just marvelous. It's a wonderful place to invite your friends. Is she...just a friend, or a very *good* friend? No, don't answer that. I shouldn't have asked. I'm just a little...surprised, that's all."

Was that kindness she saw in his eyes? Or, heaven forbid, pity? God, she was so gauche! Vesper Barnes was right about one thing, at least. She had absolutely no breeding, none at all. "Why don't I go air out another bedroom? In fact, why not the other room in your wing? Not that I—that is, maybe you'd prefer to share a—"

Her shoulders sagged. "Harrison, don't mind me. I'm running a twelve-volt mouth on a two-volt brain. You mentioned hiring a housekeeper? This might be a good time to start looking around."

The limousine arrived late that afternoon, just as they were setting out on their postprandial stroll, Cleo undertaking the excursion under duress, as usual. As limousines went, it was fairly modest. Certainly not one of those pretentious Hollywood models, but it was unmistakably a limousine.

"Harrison," she whispered, clutching his arm.

"Nick? What the devil—" He patted her hand absently, and then he began to grin. "Nick, you old son of a gun, what the devil are you doing down here?"

The front passenger door swung open. Something—or someone—was ejected. There was a cry of, "Oh, wow, a real log cabin, just like camp!" and then Cleo's attention was drawn to a long, *long,* elegant leg, in navy slacks that were obviously silk, emerging from the rear door.

Five-inch heels. They had to be all of five inches high.

"Darling, we decided to surprise you. What on *earth* are you doing in a place like this? Do you have any idea how long it took us to get here? God, I'm dying for a drink! Nick wouldn't let me open the Bollinger."

Eight

Life was far from boring, Cleo told herself as she brushed her teeth and prepared for bed that night. In fact, if it got any more *un*boring, she wasn't certain she could handle it. If she had to share her house with three strangers, she could have done with a bit more warning.

Not that she knew what she could have done with it. Put out the welcome mat?

Hardly. She might have cried a little more, eaten a little more ice cream, thrown a small tantrum.

The trouble was, she was getting entirely too comfortable in her cozy little rut. The intrusion of a woman, a child and a tough-looking, flashy-dressed man had come along just in time.

Harrison had been every bit as surprised as she was when the limo had pulled into the yard. He was good when it came to covering his feelings, but she was learning to read small signs. The tightening of his jaw. The lines between his eyebrows. That flicker of surprise that registered the instant before he could disguise it with a broad smile.

Oh, yes, she was coming to know him well.

He had mentioned meeting a woman at the airport. He hadn't said a word about the boy who'd scurried from the front seat like a flushed quail, or the swarthy man who'd climbed out from under the steering wheel.

What bothered her most—and the fact that it bothered her at all bothered her even more—was Marla Kane. Exactly where did she fit in Harrison's life? Were they kinfolks? Business acquaintances? Friends? Lovers?

So far she'd seen no sign of sexual interest on either side, only a dry peck on the lips when he'd helped her out of the car.

The boy had rolled his eyes and said, "Yuk."

Cleo had been too busy struggling to overcome surprise, curiosity and resentment, not to mention a few other emotions that didn't bear close scrutiny, to say anything.

And what about Nick Sebastiani, the driver? There was obviously some sort of relationship between the two men. They'd done that male thing—handshakes with the extra clasp. Grins and a few backslaps. He seemed pleasant enough. His clothes were a bit flamboyant—fitted purple shirt, lizard-skin belt on black jeans and matching boots with silver-capped toes—but then, he had the sort of good looks that could carry it off. She'd like to paint him, only it had been so long, her paints had probably all dried up.

Young Reynolds Kane was something else. He'd burst out of the car like a frisky spaniel puppy, sizzling with energy, brimming with curiosity. "Hey, Nick, what are those things in the edge of the water? They look like dinosaurs crawling up out of the prime—the primorbital ooze."

"Primordial," Marla corrected. "Sweetie, I told you, never preface your remarks with 'Hey.'"

"Yes, but what are they?"

Cleo had stepped in then. "Actually, they're—"

Cypress knees, she was about to say, but by then the boy was on to another question. "What's that man doing out there in the water with that cage? I bet he's a smuggler, don't you?"

"That's a—" She started to tell him about crab pots, but he was off again. What's this? What's that? Man, what are those big floppy birds?

She caught him staring at her stomach and hoped he wouldn't ask her about *that*. Helplessly, she glanced at Marla Kane, but the tall, reed-thin brunette in the navy slacks, lime green silk shirt and white blazer appeared to be arguing with Harrison about something.

Reynolds didn't ask. "I know what that is," he informed her smugly. "It's a baby. I know all about that kind of stuff. They told us in sex class how to get 'em and all." His audacious grin, complete with braces, indicated that he also knew precisely how close to the edge he could skate without getting into trouble.

Before Cleo could come up with a proper response, he'd spotted her family of mallards. "Hey, look—ducks! Can I feed 'em? We had ducks at camp last year, and we fed 'em corn. Do you have any corn?"

More questions followed before she could tell him that no, she didn't have corn but she did have birdseed, and yes, the river was really named the Alligator, and no, she'd never actually seen any alligators there herself, but from time to time they were reported in the area, and no, she didn't really know what made alligators different from crocodiles.

Her head had been spinning by the time Nick stepped in. "Round up your gear now, Rip. Your mama's tired."

Marla hadn't looked tired, Cleo remembered thinking. Irritated, perhaps, but hardly tired. No woman should look so good at the end of a two-day drive.

She heard Nick say quietly to Marla, "Has he taken his pill?"

Reynolds piped up, "Nah. I forgot it."

"Bat ears." Nick ruffled the boy's hair. Marla lifted her shoulders in a gesture too elegant to be called a shrug, and then Nick told the boy he might as well hold off until morning. "But slow down, okay? Find your blazer, hang it up and tie your shoestrings before you trip."

Judging by the amount of luggage they'd brought with them, Cleo thought they might be planning to stay all summer. Harrison reached for the two largest bags, but Nick waved him off. "I'll handle this, sir. You show Marla and the kid to their rooms."

Sir?

Cleo glanced at Harrison. "Sir?" she echoed softly.

"Yes, what is it?" he snapped without even looking at her. He was too busy looking at Marla Kane. Cleo, feeling dumpy and dowdy by contrast, decided she wasn't quite as skilled at reading faces as she'd thought.

But then, reading Harrison's face was like trying to read someone else's locked diary. It might hold a wealth of fascinating material, but unless you had the key, you'd never know what it was.

She waddled along after the parade, wondering if

she had enough food on hand, wondering where to put the two additional guests. She'd aired out the only remaining trophyless guest room, the one next to Harrison's. She had an idea young Reynolds—or Rip, as he preferred to be called—would adore trophies, the more ferocious the better. She only hoped Nick would be as easy to please.

Would he be staying? He was only the driver…wasn't he?

"Oh, man, look at those antlers!"

Cleo made it up the steps, huffing and puffing, just as the others disappeared inside. "You like those? Wait'll you see your bedroom."

"I've got antlers in my bedroom?"

She lowered her voice conspiratorially. "Honey, you've not only got antlers, you've got a bear and the skull of a longhorn bull with horns as wide as a pickup truck." She stretched her arms and wiggled her fingertips.

"Oh, man, this place is cool!"

If trophies were any indication of cool, then the place was frigid. Personally, she detested the things, but Niles had insisted on having them. Said they completed the image. Image had been important to Niles.

As far as Cleo was concerned, they were something else to be vacuumed, only not the birds. Those had to be wiped down with a damp cloth. She'd learned that the hard way, when she'd stripped half the feathers from a ring-necked pheasant. That was when they'd had their first big fight. Over a few feathers on a dead bird, of all things.

At least she no longer had to get dressed every morning under all that glassy-eyed surveillance.

Niles, claiming he'd developed an allergy to them several years ago, had moved the ones from the master suite into one of the other wings.

Nick managed everything. While Reynolds explored and Harrison gave Marla the grand tour, he made her sit down. "My mama had eleven kids, Ms. Barnes. I was number six. You shouldn't be trying to do too much at this stage. Ma always said in the last few weeks, even breathing took too much energy."

If he was curious about who she was and what she was doing in Harrison's house in this condition, he was too polite to ask. He dug out the spare bed linens when she pointed out which carton she thought they were in. They weren't, but he eventually located them. He insisted on making up the beds in the south wing and assured her that he didn't mind sharing a bath with Reynolds, and that, no, the trophies wouldn't bother them at all.

Harrison shaved for dinner. He'd gotten out of the habit of shaving twice a day. It was only one of many things that had changed since he'd come south. It occurred to him a few minutes later as he joined the others that his life had been totally structured for as long as he could remember.

Was it possible that he could have mistaken structure for substance?

Marla had brought along a Bollinger '89, which he accepted with every evidence of pleasure. He wasn't much of a champagne drinker. White wines, even good wines, gave him a hellacious headache. Either she'd forgotten, or she'd never noticed.

Nick had brought him a box of his favorite double

coronas. Don Jivan Los Lectores. At the rate of one a day, they should last him about six weeks. Naturally, he wouldn't smoke them inside, not until after Cleo had gone.

Gone. Funny thing—he had trouble picturing the lodge without her. He could picture diapers and other baby paraphernalia hanging from the antlers—he could even see cribs and playpens on the decks. But no Cleo?

No way.

Tilting his champagne flute, he watched the bubbles rise and wondered how the devil he'd got himself involved in this crazy situation. More to the point, he wondered what he was going to do about it. If he'd needed an example of just how far off course a man could swerve once he lost control of his life, he couldn't ask for a better one.

Conversation was desultory, mostly between Nick and Marla. The boy had gone to bed soon after a makeshift meal they'd all pitched in to prepare. Even Marla. She was a good sport. But then, that's why she was here.

They were all tired. Cleo was having trouble staying awake. She was usually in bed by ten. Tonight, in honor of the guests, she was evidently determined to stick it out.

Observing her without appearing to, Harrison thought about reminding her that they were his guests, not hers, and that she was under no obligation to play hostess.

But then, if he did that, either her feelings would be hurt or she'd climb back up on her high horse. Neither one of them needed the hassle. It was a battle they'd already fought to a draw. By silent mutual consent they had postponed a resolution until after the baby came.

Harrison watched her eyelids sag, fly open and then sag again as she tried to keep up with the conversation. Bless her, none of it was worth losing sleep over, especially as she'd be up at least half a dozen times during the night to go to the bathroom.

"Harrison? Harrison, wake up. Did you hear what I said? You knew I was doing the Rothstein benefit again this year, but did you read in the *Times* that we cleared nearly seventy thousand? That's net, darling, not gross. We had all the biggest corporate donors there, thanks to the latest flap about corporate welfare. The first hint of scandal and little ole Marla is off and running. I've learned to skip top management and go directly to public relations. You can't believe what a bit of bad press can do to open corporate vaults."

Harrison managed an appropriate murmur. Her tactics were no secret to him. It was one of the things he'd always admired about her, the talent for knowing what she wanted and how to go about getting it, even at his expense.

"Melba begged me to take on the children's thing next spring. They're in the middle of a nasty audit. I told her to ask me again after I've spent a few weeks at Elizabeth's, soaking in warm mud like a lazy pig. I'm flying out to Phoenix Thursday of next week."

She held out her glass for a refill. Nick reached for it, the fragile stemware incongruous in his hamlike fist. When he poured her a scant inch and a quarter, Harrison thought, amused, that if ever a man had been cut out to be a mother, it was Nick Sebastiani. When

Harrison had left New York, it was with the understanding that Nick was going to use the limo and his severance pay to set himself up in business. Harrison didn't know—nor did he want to know—if this trip with Marla was strictly business or something more personal.

He did know that his perspective, and with it his plans, had undergone a change. Thank God he hadn't actually proposed. Marriage, even the kind of marriage he'd been considering, was a serious step. The health implications for a divorced man were even worse than those for a man who had never married.

Early morning mist still blanketed the opposite shore the next day when Harrison quietly let himself out of the house. He stretched, flexing one set of muscles after another. He hadn't slept well, which was nothing new. Too much on his mind—also nothing new.

At least he hadn't woken up with a monster headache. There was something to be said for this moderation business after all.

"Hey, where ya going?"

Midstretch, with one foot up on the deck railing, he glanced around. Young Rip was strolling up from the water's edge with an empty birdseed sack in one hand, a stick in the other. Wet, muddy and grinning, he would have been a perfect model for Huck Finn if it weren't for the braces and the two-hundred-dollar shoes.

"Out."

"Mom says that's not an answer."

"Your mom's right. I'm going to run a couple of

miles before breakfast. If you want to come with me, that's fine, but I warn you, I don't talk when I'm running.''

"Why not? Because you're out of breath?"

"Because I'm thinking, da—darn it.''

"You can say dammit. My dad says it a lot. He says worse'n damn sometimes. Mom doesn't curse. She says it's a sign of a weak vo—vocallary or something. I think it means you don't know enough good words.''

They jogged along in silence while Harrison concentrated on regulating his breathing. He wasn't in quite as good shape as he'd thought, but he was getting there.

"Mom said I had to call her 'Mother.' I wanted to call her Marla. Billy Schumer calls his stepmother Rosemary. That's cool, don't you think so?''

"Not particularly. Mom's fine. Or Mother."

"Yeah, I guess.'' They jogged along for another few minutes before the boy peeled off with a casual salute. "Hey, I'm starved. I'm gonna go grub up, okay?''

Harrison had a feeling Marla was in for quite an education before she returned the boy to his father. She'd mentioned that her ex-husband was supposed to have had him between school and summer camp, but a business delay in Belgium and an epidemic of head lice at school had played havoc with their well-planned schedule.

Picking up the pace, he ran as far as the graveled road and turned back, thinking that there was something wrong when a child's life was so damned structured that even time-out depended on someone else's schedule. Funny, he'd never stopped to consider it before, maybe because as far back as he could remember, his own life had been tightly regimented. He'd been taught at an early age that time was far too valuable to waste playing. Every minute must be used constructively, either to achieve or to acquire, with emphasis on the latter.

Amazing, he mused, how a simple change of perspective could open a man's eyes. Nothing had turned out the way he'd planned it, and he was a man who'd always planned carefully and then followed those plans to the letter.

Marla had been number three—or was it four?—on his list. The stress-free wife. Had he honestly thought she'd be content to settle down in a modest log cabin at the end of a dirt road?

If he'd chosen to relocate on Sanibel Island, or even Kennebunkport, it might've worked. But then, if he'd done that, he'd have been right back in the same old circle. Within a year—two years, tops—he'd have been right back on the old familiar treadmill. He didn't know a single soul who owned property within five hundred miles of this place, and that suited him just fine. If the time ever came when he grew bored with the pace—and he didn't rule out the possibility—he could move. For now, though, he was surprisingly content.

Granted, he hadn't thought beyond his own selfish interests. When he'd made his plans, he'd been so sure Marla would leap at the chance to snag one of the world's most eligible bachelors. What an arrogant ass he'd been.

Still was, for that matter. Thank God he'd come to

his senses in time. Marla deserved far more than he'd been prepared to offer. She was a hell of a fine woman. Beautiful, intelligent, yet smart enough not to flaunt it. She was an expert when it came to dealing with people, singly or in groups. He'd seen her bring order out of chaos with the lift of a finely arched brow and the tap of a teaspoon on a microphone. It was one of the reasons she was called on so often to organize charity bashes, the other being that her own tax-deductible donation was usually in the vicinity of five figures.

It occurred to him that in some ways they were a lot alike. Polished on the surface, tough as steel underneath. She wasn't particularly good with the boy, but then, close relationships had never been his forte, either, although he liked to think he was improving in that respect. Growing, learning—a work in progress as opposed to being washed-up. Finished. Over the hill.

By the end of his run, Harrison was winded and sweaty, but invigorated. Not at all a bad way to start out the day. At least the muscles at the back of his neck weren't frozen into knots.

Nick Sebastiani, wearing green shorts and a leopard-print shirt along with silver-chained loafers and no socks, was busily polishing the limo when Harrison jogged into the yard again. He was beginning to understand why the man had occasionally griped about having to wear a uniform.

"You're keeping her in great shape," he remarked.

"She's never been on a dirt road before. Shock to her system."

"I thought by now you'd be hiring staff and looking into expanding your fleet."

"Thinking about it. Still checking out the territory."

"Sure, no point in rushing into anything. Join me for breakfast?"

"Nah, I want to check her levels before we head back."

"Plenty of time. You just got here."

Nick nodded and went back to caressing the right front fender with a chamois.

Halfway to the deck, Harrison spotted Cleo stretched out on the chaise longue, a glass of iced tea in her hand and a book on snakes in the other. The boy knelt beside her, cradling a snake shed in his hands.

"Harrison, back me up on this, will you? I say it's a rat snake. Rip insists it's a copperhead." Cleo gazed up at him, admiring the way his T-shirt clung to his sweaty body. For a man with an admitted health problem, he was a living, breathing picture of masculine fitness.

"Give me five minutes to shower and grab a cup of coffee first, will you?"

"Take all the time you need," she murmured, realizing somewhat to her surprise that she meant it. If he'd asked her for the next ten years, she would have agreed just as easily. Either her nice pink prepartum fog was clouding her judgment, or she was experiencing a few even more alarming symptoms. Such as the nest-building urge.

There was no point in calling it dinner when it was only a tray of assorted sandwiches, made and served by Nick on the front deck. He was turning out to be a real jewel. Cleo had learned that he'd once been Harrison's chauffeur, which had prompted a fresh set of questions, none of which she had voiced. What kind of man needed a full-time chauffeur? A millionaire? A politician? An international criminal?

No way. Not Harrison. And anyway, whoever he was—whoever he'd been—it was none of her business.

"There goes a sloop like the one Chad Williams bought last season." Marla waved a hand in the general direction of the river.

"More iced tea?" Nick asked Cleo.

"Thanks. You're spoiling me."

"Women need to be spoiled at a time like this. Pop said a woman's highest calling was—"

"Nicky, where's Reynolds? He didn't finish his sandwich."

"I'll check up on him. We forgot his pill again. I figured it was too late by the time I remembered it."

Cleo rubbed her aching back and wondered idly why Nick was the one to keep up with the boy's medication...and what the pills were for. He certainly appeared healthy. By the middle of the afternoon he'd gone through three changes of clothing in the process of capturing a box turtle, a mud slider and a bullfrog, all of which he'd brought to show her. She'd told him where there was a nest of baby mice, and then explained that they were too young to be separated from their mama, even if Marla would have allowed him to keep one.

Harrison, enjoying his cigar *du jour*, leaned back

in a deck chair, both feet propped on the railing, and listened to the drone of insects, the soothing sound of water lapping against the shore, the buzz of a distant outboard motor and the soft murmur of voices behind him.

Contentment. It had nothing whatsoever to do with money, power or position. Funny, a man could live thirty-seven years without learning a damned thing about life.

He gave Marla two more days, tops, before she'd be out of here. He could always tell when she was growing restless. She stroked her right thumbnail. Tapped a toe. Drank a little more than usual.

Until recently, he'd probably exhibited his own set of signals. Now, perfectly relaxed, he blew out a stream of aromatic smoke and watched it drift off to disappear in the light fog floating a few feet above the still surface of the river.

Something was bothering Cleo. He didn't think it was Marla. Considering the little they had in common, the two women got along surprisingly well.

It occurred to him that Cleo could get along with anyone. She had her own way of dealing with things. She and the boy had a mutual admiration society going between them, mostly because she took time to listen as if she were genuinely interested in what he had to say. If she hadn't been so pregnant, she'd probably be wading, fishing, climbing trees and searching for arrowheads, enjoying it every bit as much as Rip did.

His own mother, Harrison mused, would have said Cleo had no sense of propriety. She'd have been right. It was one of the things he liked about her, the total lack of pretension. One of a growing number of things.

As for his father, he wouldn't have given her the time of day. Kingston Lawless was one of the most ruthless men he'd ever known. It scared the hell out of him to realize just how much like his father he was. In another few years...

Thank God for the warning. He only hoped he'd got out in time.

It was just after midnight. Something had aroused him from a sound sleep. He checked his watch, knowing that if it was anywhere near 4:00 a.m., he wouldn't be able to go back to sleep. Four was his personal witching hour. If for any reason he roused anywhere near four, he might as well get up, shower and start his day. At his desk. With the pot of coffee Mac always had ready and waiting, knowing it would be needed.

But something had definitely brought him out of a sound sleep. If it was that damned owl he'd heard last night, the bird was history. Endangered or not, it'd be one more trophy before it ever pulled that trick again.

Tap-tap-tap. Not whoo-whoo.

Okay, it wasn't the damned owl, it was the woodpecker. Whatever it was, it was dead meat if he got his hands on it.

The hesitant sound came again. From the door?

From the door. Someone was knocking on his door. Marla.

Marla?

Oh hell, what if she wanted sex? In spite of what

he'd read about sex after a coronary, he wasn't sure he should. Wasn't even sure he could.

He knew one thing. If he did—if they did—there went another set of plans down the drain.

"Aw, hell," he muttered, throwing back the covers and reaching for his robe. He might as well give up and stop making plans, for all the good it ever did. He forked his hair back, tightened the belt on his navy silk robe and opened the door.

"Harrison, I need you. Please?"

Nine

"What's wrong? Come inside—sit down. Lie down. No, don't do that." It took him a full ten seconds to pull himself together. They were the longest ten seconds of his life.

"Harrison, I think I'm getting ready to have it. My back's been aching all day. I started having these pains, and when I got up—" She looked as if she expected him to tell her what to do.

If I were a praying man, this would be a good time to give it a shot. "Are you sure? Maybe you just pulled a muscle or—"

"Harrison? I'm sure."

They were standing in the doorway, speaking softly. He didn't know whether to carry her to his bed or head for the hospital. "I'll get Marla. She'll know what to do."

"It's probably not an emergency, only I thought—since it'll take a while—maybe we ought to get started. Would you drive me in?"

"Harrison? Cleo? What's going on?" Marla had joined them. "What are you two standing here whispering about?"

"I think I'm having my baby," Cleo said, looking miserable and a little frightened.

"Has your water broken yet?"

"Has her *what* done *what?*"

Ignoring him, Cleo nodded. "When I got out of bed."

"If it's your first, you still have plenty of time." Marla turned to Harrison. "Why don't you go wake Nick while I help her get dressed?"

"What does Nick have to do with anything?"

"Just do it," she said. Gesturing for Cleo to follow her, Marla led the way to the north wing. "I suppose you've got a bag packed, but there might be a few last-minute things you'd like to include."

Cleo caught her breath as another gripping pain began gathering low in her belly. Biting her lip, she waited for it to pass. Marla, several feet ahead of her, turned back and waited, too.

"Better now? Good. We'll have time to get a few things done before the next one hits. I'm surprised you didn't schedule a C-section so you wouldn't have to go through with all this, but then, some women prefer pain to a scar. Is there anything special I can help you pack? I can do that while you get dressed. Brush your teeth, too. It might be ages before you can do it again, and don't forget your moisturizer. Hospitals are so dry."

"Marla, would you do something else for me? There used to be a box of stationery in the wooden box on the end table in the living room. Would you look and see if it's still there, please?"

"Darling, I doubt if you'll be there long enough for that."

"Please?"

Marla shrugged. "Of course. Stationery. No

woman should go into labor without it. Don't forget your bedroom slippers.''

They made it to the hospital in thirty-three minutes. At that time of night there was little traffic, and Nick was an exceptional driver. Harrison sat in back, holding her hand. Now and then he snapped out a terse instruction. "Curve coming up—watch it. Take a right on 37. Once you cross the bridge, look for 32 and take a left. Easy, easy—no, not you, Nick. Here, let's get your feet up on the seat."

He resettled her so that she was lying against his chest, supported by his arms. When the pains came she dug her fingers into his shoulders. He winced, but he only said, "Easy, sweetheart, it won't be long now, you'll be just fine," and things like that.

Cleo couldn't believe it was finally happening. That in a matter of hours she'd be holding her baby daughter in her arms. Or her son. She didn't care which. Hadn't wanted to know because knowing would have made it too real, and after the shock, the pain and sadness of losing Niles, even though they'd been on the verge of another separation, she'd been afraid to hope.

It would be a girl. She had a really strong feeling about it. With a girl, Henry Barnes might not even be interested. He'd talked so much about the sons she and Niles would have to carry on the family law tradition, as if a daughter couldn't possibly make the grade. But then, that was Henry. And to a lesser extent, Niles.

"Harrison, do you think you can find me a stamp when we get to the hospital?" she asked, and then shut her eyes tightly as another wave of pain closed in. "Whoo! I didn't know it was going to be like this."

Harrison cradled her, stroked her back and shoulders and murmured, "Shh, it's going to be all right, everything's going to be just fine."

"But the stamp?"

"The stamp. Right. Whatever you want. Now, stop worrying."

"Easy for you to say," she scoffed. Then she laughed a little and gave in to the next surge of pain.

James Robert Niles Barnes was born just after 5:00 a.m. Six pounds, eleven ounces, twenty-two inches long, he had to be the most beautiful baby ever born, despite what the nurses all assured her were a few strictly temporary flaws.

His face was as red as a tomato. His eyes were swollen shut. Both conditions, she was promised, would clear up in a matter of days, if not hours. The fact that his head was a tad pointed was only a temporary effect of the birth process. Before she knew it he'd be looking every bit as perfect as the baby in the toilet tissue ads.

Cleo didn't care what he looked like. He was hers and he was the most precious thing on earth. Puffy-eyed or not, he recognized her. The moment she took him in her arms, he quietened down. "You and me, sweetheart. Jimmy and Mama. We're going to have a wonderful time taking care of each other, aren't we?" she whispered.

Harrison had stayed with her until after it was all over, and then he'd raced back to the house. When he returned a few hours later in his own car, he told her he had his people working on securing a cook-housekeeper.

His people. Nick or Marla? Nick, she hoped. Cleo trusted Nick's judgment where people were concerned. Any servant Marla chose would probably be one of those starchy, upper-crusty types Mrs. Barnes was so fond of, the kind who'd always made her feel inadequate. She was working on her inadequacies, but things like that took time.

Nick sent a huge bouquet of gloriosa daisies, which made her cry. And then two orderlies came in bringing enough flowers to stock every florist between Manteo and Williamston, and she cried so loud Harrison and the nurse both came rushing in, wanting to know what was wrong.

"Aw, come on now, they're supposed to make you smile," Harrison said plaintively.

"They're b-beautiful! So many— So much— Nobody ever— I don't know why you d-did it," she wailed.

"Just say thanks, and I'll say you're welcome, and we'll call it even, all right? Now, tell me about this son of yours."

So they talked about Jimmy, and she told him about her father, James Robert Larkin, who had made a name for himself in art circles back in the sixties before he'd become a victim of multiple sclerosis.

She cried a little, and then gloated while he admired her son, and then she gave him a letter to mail. "I wrote to Jimmy's grandparents. I thought they ought to know."

Harrison said, "Somehow I got the impression that

you weren't too eager to get in touch with your in-laws.''

"I'm not. I hadn't planned to tell them at all, but Niles was their only son. When it came right down to it, I couldn't *not* tell them. They might not even be interested, and that's just fine."

From the few things she'd let slip, Harrison had formed his own opinion of her in-laws. It wasn't a particularly flattering one, not that she'd said anything openly critical, either of her in-laws or her late husband. But Harrison was good at reading between the lines. To his way of thinking, she'd be a lot better off without them than with them.

He figured there wasn't much chance of that. Her late husband had been the only child of a successful father, just as he had. Successful men tended to think in terms of sons, grandsons—dynasties. King Lawless had died before it had become an issue, but Henry Barnes might be a different matter.

Cleo was obviously strapped for cash, watching every penny, counting on the sale of the lodge to give her enough to live on. He took a calculated risk. "At least now that I'm buying the lodge you won't have to worry about finances."

She pokered up, just the way he'd known she would. Pride was a funny thing. Hers had evidently taken a beating at the hands of these people, yet her innate sense of integrity had made her do what she considered the right thing. That took courage. At a time like this, when she was physically and emotionally exhausted, it wouldn't hurt to remind her that she had what it took to be a warrior.

So he did.

She sighed and said, "I know. I'm tough as old boots."

Right. Sure she was. Acting on impulse, he leaned over and brushed her lips with his. "For luck," he whispered.

She smiled that lazy, drowsy, guileless smile that had kicked the props out from under him more than once, and then, just like that, she fell asleep.

Some warrior, he thought, feeling a warmth in the region of his heart that was a symptom of something he didn't care to examine too closely. For a long time he watched her, thinking she looked tired but oddly content. The first time he'd laid eyes on her, he remembered thinking she looked tired. Tired, wary and far too defenseless for a woman living alone. Since then he'd come to know her a lot better, but some things hadn't changed.

"I didn't realize we'd be going home so soon. I've got all these books and leaflets, but, Harrison—I don't know how to take care of a baby. I've never even been around any babies."

They were approaching the turnoff. He slowed down, glanced in the mirror at the car seat, remembering what a fuss she'd made when they'd told her she couldn't hold her baby in her arms while riding in a car. "You can do anything, I'm convinced of it. You're invincible."

"I know. I'm woman, hear me roar," she said dryly.

"Is that what you call it?"

She laughed, but he heard the break in her voice. He'd never known a woman who could cry so easily over nothing at all. But then, he'd never known anyone even faintly like Cleo Barnes. While they were waiting for the orderly to bring the wheelchair after she'd been released from the hospital, he'd told her about seeing two logging trucks and several cars come to a complete stop near the foot of the bridge while a young opossum crossed the highway. He'd laughed. She'd cried.

Go figure.

"By the way, Nick and the Kanes left this morning."

"Oh, no," she wailed. "Didn't they even want to see Jimmy?"

"They saw him. Nick drove by the hospital on the way north. You were asleep and they didn't want to wake you, but they went by the nursery. Nick says send him a picture when his eyes open. Marla said it was lovely meeting you. Rip says you're going to have the devil of a time finding a bicycle helmet to fit that head."

This time she laughed. "If Rip's an example of what little boys are like, I'm not sure I'm going to survive the next few years."

"You'll do just fine," he told her, and meant it. He'd watched her with Marla's son. There'd been no pretense, no adult condescension. She'd been great with the boy. Rip had liked her for the simple reason that she'd liked him, had treated him as an individual, not as someone's kid.

Harrison could only hope that when he finally found his stress-free wife and got started on his two-point-whatever offspring, he'd have as good a relationship with them.

Watching Harrison carry her son into the house she and Niles had built in the early days of their marriage, before things had gone so terribly wrong, Cleo tried to smile but couldn't quite bring it off. At least she didn't cry. She was determined to skip the depression stage entirely. The baby blues everyone had warned her about. She'd been on an emotional seesaw for so long, all she wanted now was to ease back into her nice, comfortable rut and stay there with her baby for the foreseeable future.

But first she had to locate another nice, comfortable rut.

Well. She'd worry about that tomorrow.

When Harrison suggested she might want to lie down while he put together some lunch—it seemed he had bought out the deli counter at the supermarket—she smiled and said she thought that might be a good idea. She felt weepy again for no reason other than the fact he was being so wonderful when he was under no obligation at all, but she smiled.

And then she saw the room. The brand-new crib, complete with an array of crib toys. The bicycle, the baseball glove and bat, the fishing rod. And the flowers.... This time he'd bought out every florist east of Raleigh.

Her chin wobbled. The tip of her nose turned red. Her throat thickened until she couldn't have spoken if her life depended on it. And so she did the next best thing. She turned, baby in arms, and buried her face in his chest.

As if it were the most natural thing in the world, he embraced her. He held her there—held both of them, because she was holding Jimmy—and mur-

mured more of those sweet, meaningless words that
felt like a healing balm poured over raw wounds she
hadn't even realized she had.

"I'm sorry, I'm sorry," she whispered.

"Shh, it's all right. Everything's going to be all
right now, you're home."

Well…she wasn't, not really. They both knew it,
but it was what she needed to hear at the moment,
and so she didn't argue. Tomorrow—next week—
soon, anyway, she'd be strong enough to make plans.
If she had to send out a second barrage of résumés,
she'd do it. If she had to storm the employment office,
she would do that. There were parts of the world
where women had babies and went right back to work
in the fields. The least she could do was decide on
where she wanted to live and set the wheels in motion.

It was late when she sank down onto the sofa, exhausted from trying to make Jimmy stay awake long
enough to nurse, and then trying to find out why he
kept crying. Maybe he wasn't getting enough to eat.
Maybe she wasn't doing it right. If so, it was not from
a lack of trying. Her breasts were enormous, her nipples were tender, and she almost wished she'd decided to bottle-feed him, but there were problems with
that, too, or so she'd heard.

He'd finally erupted in a noisy belch and fallen
asleep in her arms. She'd put him down and stood
watching him sleep for twenty minutes before going
out to the kitchen to find something to eat.

Oh Lord, Harrison had restocked the freezer. Gallons and gallons of ice cream in every imaginable

flavor, and not a single one of them tempted her the least bit.

She could hear him in the living room talking on the phone. He sounded different—edgier. More like the man who had first turned up at her front door and announced that he intended to buy her house. She waited until he hung up, then picked up her plate of cold pasta and fruit and wandered in to join him.

With his shirt unbuttoned, a dark stubble shadowing his jaw, he looked almost as tired as she felt. He reached over and picked a few grapes off her plate.

"All settled now?"

"Harrison, what if I'm doing it all wrong? I wish babies came with a set of instructions."

"I bet you've never read a complete set of instructions in your life." He'd taken the chair. The sofa was hers by unspoken agreement.

"How could you possibly know that?"

"What, that you don't read instructions? Oh, I dunno, just a shot in the dark."

"You mean because I don't read contracts, either?"

Instead of answering, he asked if there was any more pasta in the kitchen. She shoved her plate across the coffee table. Suddenly, she wasn't hungry.

Over the next several days, clocks and calendars were useless. James the Despot, as Harrison had taken to calling him, ruled the household with an iron hand. Or rather, with an iron set of lungs.

Cleo was exhausted but secretly proud. Her son might be small, but he knew how to make his presence felt. "Sorry about last night. And the one before that. If you'd like to get out of our agreement, it's not too late,'' she offered one morning when they met, bleary-eyed after another sleepless night.

He could have closed his door and not heard a thing. Instead, he brought her cocoa and sandwiches in the middle of the night and lingered to see that she finished the last drop and crumb.

"Well?" she challenged.

"No way."

Which was just as well. She'd given her word he could have the house. Besides, she didn't know what she would do without him. Him, not his rent money. She hadn't cashed a single check, partly out of pride, but mostly out of something else. It wasn't his money she wanted, it was the man himself.

And if that wasn't postpartum dementia, she didn't know what to call it.

"Fine. Just thought I'd ask."

"Fine." He crossed his arms over his chest. "Take as long as you need. I think I've finally located a cook-housekeeper. She's a Mrs. Davis, widow— worked at a bed-and-breakfast on the beach until it closed down at the end of last season. I think you'll like her."

Cleo murmured something to the effect that it hardly mattered whether she did or not, she wouldn't be here much longer.

"Oh, and by the way, I'm expecting a delivery in the next few days."

She nodded but didn't comment. Why in the world should she resent the fact that another woman would be moving in? It wasn't even her house any longer. At least, not completely hers. Besides, she really was getting tired of dusty floors and deli food, and as wonderful as he was, Harrison was not a domestic creature. "That's nice," she murmured, feeling every bit as cheerful as a lost lamb.

Harrison narrowed his eyes, shook his head and left to go feed her crows. It was another of the duties he'd taken over since she'd come home from the hospital.

Three days later a truckload of equipment and office furniture was delivered. Cleo knew how to use a computer. Hated the things—hated the jargon that went with them—but at least she'd learned to find her way around a keyboard.

Harrison's new computer was no simple PC. There was also a copier and an old-fashioned metal file cabinet. The fancy device in his hand was in case of a power failure or a terrorist EMP attack, he told her, and then had to explain what an electromagnetic pulse was and how it could affect all electronic equipment. He went on to describe a weapons system under development that was based on the same principle, his eyes lighting up like a kid with a brand-new toy. She stopped listening about halfway through the description and contented herself with watching the way he used his hands when he talked.

They were beautiful hands. Strong, nicely shaped, with just the right amount of black hair. Sexy hands.

He was saying something about targeting and directing radio frequencies, and she wondered what kind of businessman would be interested in something like that. Someone in the business of corporate espionage? An international spy?

Although why any spy would be interested in monitoring snowbird traffic on the sleepy old Alligator River was a mystery to her.

But then, so was Harrison. A mystery. Had been from the very first, only she'd gradually gotten used to him. Come to depend on him. Come uncomfortably close to falling in love with the man, if she was honest with herself, and that was the scariest thought of all.

"Do you have anything to do with the bombing range?" She'd been watching him set up his equipment, listening to the rich sound of his voice, not the words he spoke, and keeping one ear open in case Jimmy woke up.

"The what?"

"Bombing range. At Stumpy Point. Or any of those other places like—you know. Camp LeJeune? Cherry Point? There are a lot of military establishments in the area."

"Don't tell me, let me guess. We're past the crying stage, past the ice-cream binges, past the sleeping stage. We're now entering the stage of—what? Postpartum paranoia?"

"Oh, for heaven's sake, ask a simple question… Well, what was I to think with all this talk about electromagnetic gizmos that can shut down the whole civilized world?"

Maybe he was right. Maybe she was paranoid.

"I'm not a spy. Neither am I an international terrorist, nor a science fiction writer. I have a Ph.D. in electronics. I also have a liberal arts degree and a masters in business administration."

"Oh."

"Satisfied? I assure you, I'm perfectly harmless."

Harmless? Not in a million years. However, she

was too embarrassed to apologize, much less ask him what a man in his prime with all those qualifications and no visible means of support was doing in a place like this.

He continued to hook up his fancy gadgets, rearrange various pieces of furniture and crawl around plugging various pieces of equipment into various strips and mysterious boxes with blinking red and green lights.

Cleo continued to admire his shoulders, his neat behind and his long, square-tipped fingers. She continued to tell herself it was time to leave, even if she had to move in with Tally again, heaven forbid. Tally's tiny apartment was scarcely big enough for one, much less two adults and a baby.

The resonant sound of the newly installed doorbell echoed through the house. Actually, it was a brass ship's bell beside the door, something Harrison had acquired while she was in the hospital. The lodge was gradually taking on less and less of Niles's personality and more of Harrison's.

"Probably our new housekeeper," Harrison muttered. He backed out from under a massive new desk and dusted off his hands, further indication that the woman was desperately needed. Cleo had meant to run the vacuum, she really had, only she hated the clumsy machine with a passion, and Jimmy hated the noise.

"I'll go," she said. "I need to look in on the baby, anyway."

Ada Davis was a godsend. Small, neat and competent, she was a wealth of information, which she kept to herself unless asked, about everything from colicky babies to diaper rash to keeping rat snakes out of the house by cleaning the mice out of the utility room. Things, she stated in her no-nonsense manner, a body learned when they lived in the country.

She didn't live in. She had her own home in East Lake across the bridge, with five cats and a garden that needed her care. Dietary restrictions didn't faze her. She was a plain Southern country cook who could manage quite well, if she had to, without the enhancement of either butter or bacon grease.

After the first week, things were going so smoothly that Cleo came dangerously close to drifting back into her same old pattern. Putting off today anything that could be put off until tomorrow. Or the next day. Or the day after that.

She looked after Jimmy, celebrated each new accomplishment, snapped beans, peeled potatoes and made a stab of reading the classifieds in the newspapers that came for Harrison. Not that she particularly cared what jobs were available in New York or London.

The London *Times?*

Mercy. She'd never known anyone who actually subscribed to the London *Times.* And she'd thought Niles was sophisticated.

Actually, it was Niles who'd thought Niles was sophisticated. She had finally reached the conclusion that a large part of his problems stemmed from the fact that he'd been told all his life he was designated by birth for greatness. And greatness hadn't happened. Instead, he had barely scraped through law school and then married a woman his parents considered socially inferior, partly because she happened to think he was wonderful, and partly to escape marriage to a woman just like his mother.

He'd been a disappointment to his father, who hadn't failed to let him know it. Frustrated because there was no real substance to sustain his exaggerated self-image, Niles had taken it out in various forms of meanness and self-destruction.

Harrison had a satellite dish installed. From habit, Cleo started to object to his high-handedness, but then, the house was as good as his. The fact that she was still there meant only that they weren't yet ready for closing. Which was all very convenient for her, but all the same, she felt guilty. She kept asking about it. He kept coming up with reasons why they needed more time.

"Look at it as joint custody," he said with the teasing light in his eyes that was more and more in evidence lately.

To think she'd once compared his eyes to ice on granite.

"Yes, well...I've been looking. Mrs. Davis brought me a copy of the *Virginian Pilot* and the *Raleigh News and Observer*. Just as soon as I find a job opening and a decent, affordable place to stay, Jimmy and I will go check it out."

"Don't rush into anything." Harrison was hanging a wall shelf in Jimmy's room. Marla had sent a monogrammed sterling cup from Tiffany. Nick had sent an autographed baseball. Tally had sent an enormous teddy bear. The shelf was slightly crooked, but Harrison was so proud of his newfound carpenter skills,

Cleo didn't have the heart to mention it. Evidently, it took more than three degrees to master basic household carpentry.

He had bought a flock of rocking chairs, one for each deck, one for the living room and one for her bedroom.

"Harrison, this has got to stop!" she'd told him. "Have you lost your mind? I can't accept all this—this—"

"Furniture? I happen to like rocking chairs. Are you trying to tell me I can't have rocking chairs in my house?"

Of course she wasn't telling him that. She didn't know what she was trying to tell him, any more than she knew what he was trying to prove. Honestly, it was as if they were playing some crazy game and neither one of them knew the name of the game, much less the rules.

Jimmy loved the chairs. She rocked him and nursed him and sang to him—he was too young to realize she couldn't carry a tune. Harrison was too polite to mention it. Wherever they happened to be, he was usually somewhere nearby if he wasn't in his office doing whatever it was he did with all that equipment.

As it happened, all three of them were on the front deck when Cindy Minter arrived.

They heard the car long before it drove into the clearing. "You expecting anyone?" Harrison, kneeling beside the front steps, was setting out tomato plants. She could have told him that his plants were too leggy and droopy, and it was too late in the season to be setting them out anyway, but he'd just discovered gardening and now he was on a tomato kick. He ate tomatoes three times a day, claiming some sort of newly discovered health benefit.

The next thing he was likely to discover would be a skin rash from too much acid, but you couldn't tell the man anything. Oddly enough, his stubbornness and bossiness no longer bothered her.

"It's probably another stray." There'd been two people just last week who'd shown up, wanting to know if the road went any farther, and if not, why not. She'd told them that it was a private road, but they were welcome to get out and explore on foot, and of course when Harrison heard about it, he insisted on calling a security company to come out and give an estimate.

The small red rental swerved into the clearing in a spray of pine straw, coming to a stop within inches of Harrison's Rover. Even with all the windows closed, Cleo could hear the loud bass beat of the radio.

Harrison rose, dusted off his hands and waited. "Get in the house," he said quietly. There was something distinctly make-my-dayish in his attitude.

Clutching Jimmy protectively to her breast, Cleo was almost at the door when she glanced back over her shoulder in time to see a petite redhead in wrap-around sunglasses stumble out of the car.

"Cindy? Cindy Minter?" What in the world was a secretary from Barnes, Barnes, Wardell and Barnes doing here?

Ten

"You come back here, Cleo Barnes, I want my deed!" the woman screeched. Wearing a royal blue, body-hugging dress with a skirt that was barely decent, she wobbled her way toward the front deck, her high heels sinking into the dirt with each unsteady step. Harrison wondered if she was drunk or simply demented.

She was crying. Hysterically. Damn it all to hell, not another one, he thought. If this was an example of stress-free living, he might as well be back in New York.

Cleo moved warily to the edge of the deck, the infant cradled securely in one arm. She looked more concerned than alarmed. "Cindy, what on earth is wrong? What are you doing here? Are you hurt?"

"No, I'm not hurt! Yes, of course I am, what did you expect?"

Harrison's gaze ricocheted back and forth between the two women. He wondered if what he was witnessing was some bizarre Southern female rite of passage.

Reaching out with her free hand, Cleo helped the other woman up the last two steps. "Watch the cracks, they're rough on heels. What are you doing here, anyway? How did you know where to find me?''

"Is this Niles's baby?" The redhead removed her sunglasses, dropped them, stepped on them, staggered and peered at the small bundle in Cleo's arms. "Aaw, Ni-iles," she wailed.

"I think you'd better sit down. Are you sick? You look awful."

That was his Cleo, Harrison thought, amusement diluting his irritation. Tactful to a fault.

As it turned out over the next several minutes, Cindy Minter, legal secretary with the firm of Barnes, Barnes, Wardell and Barnes, had come in search of a deed to a house she owned and wanted to sell.

"But why on earth would your deed be here?"

"He never gave it to me, that's why. He kept promising he would, but he never did."

"Who never gave it to you? Who kept promising to do what?"

"Niles! Who do you think? He said it was with his papers somewhere, and he'd give it to me as soon as he ran across it, but he never did, and then you came back, and then he died, and they put everything under lock and key. Old Henry wouldn't even let me in his office, and I w-w-*worked* there!"

Harrison extricated the baby from Cleo's arms, ushered the two women into the living room and left them to hash things out while he put Jimmy down for a nap. The sound of female voices, one increasingly calm, the other increasingly shrill, followed him into the north wing.

Ada Davis poked her neat gray head out the kitchen

door as he passed. "What's going on? Sounds like raccoons fighting over a garbage can."

"Pretty close. How about making a pot of coffee. I think we might need it."

"Real, fake or half and half?"

"Real."

Cleo drank decaf. Because he was still in the process of "decaffeinating"—down to a one-third, two-thirds mix and holding—he still had both kinds on hand.

Jimmy was fretful but having trouble keeping his eyes open. "You've got a lot to learn, son. No matter how much you think you know, there's a whole other universe out there waiting to blindside you. Yeah, I'd fuss about it, too, if I were you." Gently, Harrison lowered the drowsy infant to the crib, then pulled the sheet up and waited to see if it was going to get kicked off again.

He tilted the lamp shade so it shone on Cleo's vast bed instead of on the crib. The bed looked inviting. He pictured her curled up in the middle of the king-size mattress and thought, What a waste.

It wasn't the bed he was thinking about.

He was tempted to hide out in his office until things settled down, but he figured it was about time he took control. When it came to scouting out the enemy in a purely social setting, he was among the best. Hell, he *was* the best.

Poor Cleo. Either she was dumb as a post, or she didn't want to admit what had been going on right under her nose.

She wasn't dumb. A little naive in some respects—more than a little—but never dumb. He was coming to believe she had a bone-deep kind of wisdom that was rare among the people he knew.

Minter and Barnes had obviously had an affair. Either a quick, hot one or a long-term one. No man who'd ever had an affair could miss the signs. And Harrison had. Several. One at a time, and with varying degrees of satisfaction.

The redhead was trouble. She obviously didn't know how the game was played. She could have her damned deed—she could have the deed to a dozen houses—but one thing she couldn't do was hurt Cleo.

"Want me to take it in?" Mrs. Davis inquired when he stopped by the kitchen again.

"Thanks, I'll do it. Better set another place for dinner."

Her expression spoke volumes.

As did the look on Cleo's face when he carried in the tray. Things were obviously no closer to being resolved. As the redhead had taken his chair, he turned toward the rocking chair, but Cleo reached up and caught his hand, drawing him down onto the sofa beside her. She didn't say a word. Didn't have to. Her eyes said it for her. *Please—I need you. Stay by me.*

He hoped his own message was as clear. *Relax, I'm here now.*

The familiar scent of soap, shampoo and baby powder threw him off course for only a few seconds before, calling on his rusty negotiating skills, he tendered the first question. "Ms. Minter, is there any particular reason why you'd expect to find your deed here instead of with Mr. Barnes's other personal papers?"

She blinked several times. The woman had truly

remarkable eyelashes and knew how to use them. "We were here when he gave it to me. I thought maybe he just forgot."

Cleo leaned forward, looking puzzled. "When who gave what to you?"

"When Niles gave me the house."

At the soft sound of Cleo's indrawn breath, Harrison forced himself to press on. Better a clean, deep cut than a series of smaller, ragged ones. "Am I correct in assuming the late Niles Barnes gave, sold or otherwise deeded you a house, yet he failed to give you the actual deed?" He didn't allow her time to answer. "And you believe Mrs. Barnes might know where this deed can be found? Is that it?"

Nice going, Lawless. Why not just hit her over the head with it?

"I don't understand, Cindy. Why would my husband give you a house? Was it something you two were involved with at work?"

Harrison intervened. Covering her hand with his, he said, "I think we can agree that it was an involvement, but not necessarily confined to work, am I right, Ms. Minter?"

"Cindy? Is there something you're not telling me? I know you worked for Niles—"

"Actually, for Niles and Pierce both, but Pierce was seeing that woman from accounting."

"Yes, but...a house?"

"Let it go, Cleo," Harrison murmured. He'd changed his mind. He would pay the woman off and get rid of her. Anything was better than watching her undermine, brick by brick, whatever was left of Cleo's self-respect.

Cindy sneezed. Watery streaks of blue mascara seeped onto her cheeks. She sneezed six times in a row, and Cleo got up and found her a box of tissues.

"Thank you. It's those adibals. They always bake be sdeeze."

The animals made her sneeze. She was allergic to the trophies. According to Cleo, her late husband, the philandering bastard, had removed the trophies from the master bedroom when he'd developed an allergy to them.

Or rather, when his mistress had started sneezing at the wrong time. Bloody hell.

"How did you know where to find me?"

"Cleo," he said, wanting to head her off. If she didn't get it by now, she wasn't going to. Some women could look the truth in the eye and still refuse to accept it. He'd wanted her to face it, get over it and move on, but she seemed determined to do it the hard way.

"Pierce told me you were here. He talked to that woman you worked for in Chesapeake, and—"

"I know, he called. But Tally wouldn't have told him where I was. She knew I didn't want—that is, she wouldn't."

"Pierce is smarter than most people think. One of these days he'll be a partner. Now that Niles is gone—"

"But why would Niles give you a house in the first place? I mean, I know Henry Barnes had a few rentals, but—"

"Henry? He's a slumlord. Niles would never have offered me one of those awful places."

"Yes, but—"

"Cleo, just let it drop, okay? If Ms. Minter thinks there's a deed here that belongs to her, why don't I look through a few of those boxes and see if I can find it?"

"Yes, but—"

Until this moment, Cleo hadn't realized that in spite of everything, she'd still clung to a few illusions. Niles had been weak. He'd been cruel, both verbally and physically, but somewhere deep inside her she'd held fast to the fragile belief that at least he'd been faithful. He had sworn as much when he'd begged her to come back after the first time she'd left him, otherwise she never would have agreed. Promiscuity these days was too dangerous.

"Well...shoot," she whispered. No wonder whenever she suggested spending a weekend here he'd claimed he'd invited clients down for a few days.

With every shred of dignity she could summon, she said, "Niles was my husband. I don't believe I care to discuss this matter further."

"You walked out on him. What did you expect him to do, join a monastery? And I'm not going anywhere until I find my deed." The redhead was sulky, angry and beginning to sober up. It was not a happy combination. "Niles promised me that house, and anyway, who're you to talk? You're living here with another man. I bet Niles isn't even your baby's father. I bet—"

Under Harrison's piercing regard, she caught her breath and snapped her mouth shut. CEOs had quailed before such a look. Entire boards of directors had been routed by such a look.

Cindy Minter faltered. She didn't surrender. One

quick, calculating look and she began weeping again, but he was an old hand at dealing with weeping women by now.

Cleo, looking hurt but dry-eyed, was twisting her fingers. Harrison covered both her hands with one of his own. He waited. From the kitchen came the sounds of dinner preparation. From outside came the sound of a whippoorwill and the distant popping noise of a small outboard motor.

Leaning back against the deep cushions, he drew Cleo closer against his side, feeling strong, feeling protective—not to mention somewhat curious as to how she was going to handle today's revelation. Hard to believe she hadn't known, but then in some ways, she was far too trusting for her own good.

Cindy sniffed, sobbed and mopped, tossing the damp tissues onto the floor. Harrison waited, unmoved, curious as to what she would try next. Minter's tears didn't faze him. A single one from Cleo could turn him inside out. Emotions, especially the feminine variety, had been a mystery to him ever since he'd first discovered that girls were different from boys, but he was beginning to catch on to a whole new dimension.

They searched. Cleo couldn't remember exactly where she'd put the things from Niles's safe, so they went through all the cartons, and then went through them again. Harrison and Cleo did. He refused to allow Minter to join in the search. Relegated to the chair he had come to think of as his own, she watched, alternately sneezing and weeping.

''That security outfit I called had damned well better get on the ball,'' he muttered, carefully folding a patchwork quilt and two pillow shams.

''People like to explore along the river. There aren't all that many roads they can use.''

''Cleo, you can't invite strangers onto your property these days. Not everybody's going to admire the view, thank you for your hospitality and leave.''

''So far they have. No, I've already gone through that box. It's only old books.''

''Give up. All we have to go on is her word. There might not even be a house.''

''Yes, but if there is, and it belongs to her and she needs to sell it...''

''Did anyone ever try to sell you a bridge in Brooklyn?''

''I've always wanted to own a bridge. Why, do you have one to sell?''

Cleo watched as his fist approached her face. Two months ago she would have flinched. Now she smiled. He touched her chin with his knuckles, his eyes crinkling in that way he had of not quite smiling. One touch and she was reduced to a puddle of melted candle wax. Not even Niles in the early days had affected her this way.

''Haven't you found it yet?'' came a plaintive whine from across the room.

''Not yet,'' they chorused, and then their eyes met again, this time in shared amusement. Cleo told herself not to be so darn gullible. Bridges were one thing. For a woman in her situation to fall in love with any man, much less a man like Harrison Lawless, was terminally stupid.

* * *

The deed still had not been found by dinnertime. While Cleo nursed Jimmy and settled him in his crib, and Mrs. Davis put the finishing touches on the evening meal, Harrison entertained their guest. Cleo wondered what on earth they found to talk about and was ashamed to feel a vicious little twist of jealousy.

After dinner, she wandered out onto the front deck. To think she had driven down intending only to pack, put the house on the market and find herself another place to live before the baby came.

What had happened to her? She'd never had trouble making decisions before. Other than the decision to leave Niles that first time and, later, the decision to go back to him.

This was different. There was nothing holding her here. No vows, no promises. No more hopes, much less dreams.

The truth was, there was only Harrison. Wealthy, arrogant, sweet, klutzy, impractical, bossy, mysterious—she could think of several other adjectives, but the one that worried her most was…sexy. With a brand-new baby, the last thing any sane woman should be thinking of was sex. If her body didn't stop pumping out all these crazy hormones, she was going to do something really, really stupid.

Sex. Great Scott, she hadn't even thought this much about sex when she was married. It was simply something that happened several times a week—mostly pleasant, sometimes not. Usually ''not'' after Niles had been drinking.

Or after he'd started sleeping with his secretary, she thought with a quiet sort of bitterness, but surprisingly little hurt. She was way past the point when anything

Niles had done could hurt her. The knowledge felt good.

She supposed it had been her fault, the fact that sex had usually been disappointing, for her at least. Niles said it was. She'd thought it was just another of his taunts designed to make her feel inferior but perhaps he'd been right. Perhaps she simply didn't have it in her to satisfy a man. She was an artist. At least, she'd once had ambitions to be one. Maybe artists sublimated their passions in order to translate them into their work.

Ha. Any latent artistic impulses she still harbored had to do with nude models. Male nude models. Male nudes with wide shoulders, long, lean limbs, square-tipped fingers and crinkly smiles.

The screen door behind her slammed. Ada Davis said good-night, and that she'd see if she could find some fresh peaches on the way to work tomorrow.

"That would be lovely," Cleo murmured, still caught up in a dream of seeing Harrison sprawled across a model stand wearing a loincloth and her dressed in a smock and nothing else.

Ada's rusty pickup truck rattled off into the dusk. Cleo leaned her head back, closed her eyes and tried to recapture her dreams, but the soft murmur of voices from inside the house kept interfering.

She had invited Cindy to stay the night. What else could she have done? She'd lent her a nightgown—a granny gown, white cotton with eyelet trim—and tried to ignore her look of disdain. Mrs. Davis had made up the room Nick had used. There were several trophies there, but darned if she was going to take the things down.

Harrison had accused her of being a pushover. He was probably right. She was getting better, but she still had a long way to go. There'd been a time when she'd had the gumption to fight for what she wanted, but most of the fight had been knocked out of her, first by dropping out of school to take care of her father after her mother had run off and left him. Then by falling for a charmer who could talk the devil into giving up his horns.

After years of sharing a three-story mansion with the in-laws from hell and with a husband who beat her—who kept promising to get help, but who never did—she didn't have a whole lot of gumption left.

"What a jerk you were, Niles," she whispered. "What a fool I was to have loved you."

But she had Jimmy. Without Niles, she would never have had Jimmy. And as much as she might wish things could be different, life was what it was. Deal with it, her father would have said.

After another largely sleepless night, Harrison showered, dressed and went in search of breakfast. Ada was a gem. The woman had more common sense than most CEOs he'd known. Business smarts was one thing. Plain old common sense was…entirely too uncommon.

"Is that bacon and eggs I smell?"

"Nope. Same as yesterday. Oatmeal. Got you some fresh peaches, though."

"With cream?" Cleo appeared in the doorway, looking about sixteen years old, except for her eyes. One of these days he was going to lift the shadows from those clear amber depths.

"If the good Lord had wanted cream on peaches, He'd a made 'em that way."

"Right. And his pigs would be swimming in a sea of barbecue sauce. I detect a conspiracy here." He grinned at Cleo. "Where's your friend?"

"If you mean Cindy, she's probably still sleeping. I expect she'll have a headache."

"That's putting it mildly. Have some oatmeal. You're still eating for two, remember."

The phone rang. Mrs. Davis said, "Barnes-Lawless residence," and handed it across the table.

Harrison spoke his name, listened briefly, then excused himself. "I'll take it in my office."

"Sounded important. We used to get some o' them tycoons at the bed-and-breakfast. Lot of 'em around these days. What's yours do? Real estate or politics?"

Cleo choked on her coffee. "He's not mine, he's only staying here until we close on the sale."

"Fine. None o' my business."

"Mrs. Davis—"

"Folks these days don't live like we did in my day, but that's all right. Things always evens out in the long run."

Before Cleo could think of a response, Cindy stumbled into the kitchen. "My head's killing me. Would somebody please turn off the sun?" She'd made a stab at applying makeup, but it didn't cover the shadows under her eyes, the furrows between her brows or her red and swollen nose. "I told you not to put me in that old room. I sneezed all night long. I hate those old heads! Why would any man want to decorate his house with dead animals, I ask you?"

"You want coffee or tea?" Ada Davis asked. Demanded was more like it. "Tea's better for what ails you."

Cindy sent her a malevolent look. "Lady, you don't have the least idea what ails me, so don't go giving me any of that holier-than-thou crap."

"Like I said, things always evens out," the housekeeper sniffed.

Cleo said nothing. Her breasts were aching. It was time to nurse Jimmy. She wondered if she would ever get enough of nursing him, holding him, gazing down at that eager little face, watching him clench and unclench those tiny hands. His appetite had practically doubled since he'd left the hospital. At this rate, he'd soon be joining them at the table, demanding his share of oatmeal.

She rose, rinsed her dishes and put them in the dishwasher. "If anyone needs me, I'll be on the back deck."

"Don't you let them mosquitoes bite that boy."

"I won't. If they're bad, we'll come back inside."

"You might as well know, I broke one of your stinking old animals. I threw blankets over the ugly old things so I could get some sleep, but one of them came loose. It's probably fallen to the floor by now."

Cleo sighed. She hated the wretched things, too, but if anyone was going to destroy them, it wasn't going to be some sniveling little husband-stealing bimboette. She'd trash them herself. Or maybe she could claim they were fixtures—like the kitchen appliances—that went with the sale of the house.

It was Harrison who discovered the hidden safe. Not the one in the master bedroom. Cleo had already emptied that. It had been practically empty anyway, only a few dollars, a tiny key she couldn't identify and an old address book.

After breakfast he'd gone to the guest room, surveyed the damage and intercepted Cleo on her way to change and feed a hungry baby. "You want it up or down?"

"The bear? You can take it down and throw it away for all I care. Or give it to some poor fellow who needs dead animals to boost his male ego."

Harrison was grinning when he headed for the utility closet to collect a ladder and whatever household tools he might need. Interesting take on the male ego. She might be onto something.

Or maybe she was still in the process of reappraising her late husband. God knows, she had grounds to despise the jerk.

Five minutes later he charged into her bedroom, came to a dead stop and stared. "I'm sorry—I should've knocked. I'll just..."

He swallowed hard, wondered fleetingly if this was another of those dreams that had been plaguing him lately. He hadn't had *that* kind of dream in nearly twenty years.

Their eyes met and held. The light from the window was at her back, casting one side of her face in shadow. The dress she was wearing—it was yellow, with flowers—was open from the waist up. Never in his life had he seen anything so beautiful. Even in the indirect light he could see her nipples. They were large, dark and proud. One was still wet where it had slipped from the sleeping baby's mouth.

God knows, there was nothing even faintly carnal

about the scene. It took him nearly a full minute to realize there was nothing carnal about what he was feeling, either.

At least, that wasn't all he was feeling.

"I found—I brought—"

She glanced at the sleeping infant, pulled the edges of her dress together and rose. "Shh, let me put him down."

He waited, rocked by feelings he'd never expected, didn't know how to handle and sure as hell didn't welcome. When she took his hand to lead him from the bedroom, it was all he could do not to jerk away, but he didn't.

It wasn't electricity. It wasn't one of those tired old clichés songwriters wrote about in ballads. It was more like recognition. As if he were meeting for the first time someone he'd known all his life.

Harrison had a feeling he was in way over his head.

Cleo turned away from the crib and said, "Now, what's the trouble? If the thing's broken, just throw it away. Drop it in the river—or no, I don't reckon that's legal. How do you dispose of a dead bear, anyway?"

"The bear's not the problem. It's what the bear was hiding. Maybe you'd better come check it out."

Eleven

Cleo picked one of the envelopes from among those scattered about on the table. "C.M. Do you suppose…could that be Cindy Minter?"

"Open it and see."

"I'm almost afraid to find out."

Harrison didn't much blame her. A wall safe was one thing. A secret cache was another. He had a bad feeling about this.

They were in his office. When Harrison had pried the flat metal case from where it had been wedged behind the trophy, Cleo had remembered the tiny key she'd found in the wall safe. It had taken her nearly half an hour to recall which carton she'd dropped it into.

Cindy was in the living room, nursing her headache and polishing her toenails. The radio droned softly in the kitchen, where Mrs. Davis was brisking around, making lunch. *Brisking* was a new verb Cleo had coined to describe the way the woman moved. Old Noah Webster couldn't have done better, Harrison had told her the first time he'd heard it. They'd both laughed. It occurred to him that he'd laughed more with Cleo Barnes than he'd ever laughed with any other woman he'd ever known.

Neither of them was laughing now. "Well? Are

you going to open it, or are we going to go on playing guessing games?''

"Here goes.'' She opened the manila envelope and cautiously peered inside. "It looks like a deed of trust. Commonwealth of Virginia, township of—''

She glanced up, her look both puzzled and injured. "He gave her a house,'' she said plaintively. "I had to live with his parents. They hated me. And he gave her a house.''

For long moments there was only the rustle of paper and the sound of two people breathing. Out in the kitchen, a George Strait ballad gave way to the weather and news report. *''—percent chance of showers, clearing after midnight, meanwhile, the search for William Clayton, who escaped from—''*

"Poor Cindy,'' Cleo said softly.

Poor Cindy? If Harrison had thought he was beginning to understand the way her mind worked, he'd been dead wrong.

"At least now she can sell it.''

"May I?'' He slid the document across the table and scanned it quickly. As far as he could see it was a simple, straightforward deed from Niles H. Barnes to one Cynthia Wells Minter. "Do you want to give it to her?''

Cleo glanced up, and he was struck all over again by the feeling that had come over him when he'd seen her nursing her baby. Something larger than lust, and a great deal harder to cope with.

"It's hers. We have to give it to her. What I can't understand is why Niles didn't give it to her before.''

"What's beginning to concern me even more is why the thing was hidden. A man keeps important papers in a safe or in a bank vault. I imagine he had both. What kind of papers would be kept in a place where no one would ever think of looking for them? Any ideas about that?''

She shook her head. The wariness was back again. As much as he hated to see it, he couldn't much blame her. He had a nasty feeling about where all this was leading. The seven initialed manila envelopes they'd found. The ledger that was with them—he'd thought at first it was an address book, but a cursory glance had revealed only initials with a string of numbers beside each one.

It was enough. More than enough, if what he suspected proved right, to destroy the lives of at least six people.

''You want to see what's inside the other envelopes?'' It was her call. Barnes had been her husband.

She sighed. ''I guess we'd better.''

But it was obvious she was every bit as reluctant as he was. It felt a bit like sifting through a dead man's garbage.

''Did you ever have one of those days that seemed to last forever? I haven't accomplished a single thing all day, yet I'm as tired as if I'd hung a whole gallery and then run a marathon.''

Harrison chuckled, relieved that she'd come through it as well as she had. They were both stretched out on the back deck, watching storm clouds roll in from the southwest. The hammock was back in place. He was in it.

''Never having done either, I wouldn't know. I'd

say looking after Jimmy would be enough to exhaust a platoon.''

Not to mention dealing with the mistress of a late husband and learning that that same husband, aside from being an abusive, two-timing sot, had been a blackmailing bastard who had held the deed to his mistress's house over her head in case she should ever decide to reveal a few of his dirty little secrets.

To put it politely.

''I feel sorry for her.''

He twisted around to stare at her. ''You *what?*''

''Cindy. I really do. I didn't know any of those other people—the man in the newspaper clipping or the ones in the negatives or any of the others.''

One envelope had held a strip of 35 mm negatives, black-and-white and hard to interpret, but Harrison had no doubt they were incriminating. Another envelope had held an audiotape, which they hadn't yet been able to play. The other four had held letters, memos, a bank statement and a photo taken in a night club showing a couple in a fairly intimate pose. An older man and a woman who looked barely out of her teens.

He wasn't sure even now that Cleo fully understood the significance of what they'd found, but a cursory examination of the ledger had made it pretty clear that Barnes had been bleeding the poor devils for months before he died. Years, in a couple of cases.

''What are you going to do with it?'' he asked her now.

''With the letters and pictures?'' They had already given Cindy the deed. She'd been embarrassingly grateful. She'd ended up bawling again, and Cleo had held her, comforted her.

Harrison had stalked off in disgust. Kindness was one thing. There was such a thing as taking it too far.

"I'll burn them."

"Want to tell me why?"

"I don't know—maybe because it's the easiest thing to do. I just want it to be finished. It's not as if I knew any of these people."

Harrison didn't, either. However, he had an idea they'd appreciate knowing the sword of Damocles no longer hung over their collective heads.

He nodded. It was her call. And she was right— there was no point in digging up old skeletons. "Rest in peace," he murmured.

"I know you think I'm crazy, but I really do feel sorry for her. For Cindy, I mean. She was in love with Niles when he married me. She wanted to marry him, but his folks wouldn't let him. They had this other woman picked out for him to marry."

"You?"

"Mercy, no. I was nobody. That's why he married me, to get back at them."

"People don't marry for revenge."

"Niles did. He told me so, once when he was— when we were having a—a disagreement. My family isn't even from Virginia. They were from the western part of North Carolina. You know what they call North Carolina, don't you?"

"Land of beginnings?" He'd seen the motto somewhere.

"That, too, but somebody said once it was a vale of humility between two mountains of conceit. I don't know about South Carolina, but it's true about Virginia. At least about people like the Barneses, who've been there forever. They were English. My folks were Irish. I think my granddaddy was a blacksmith. My parents were both artists. Late hippy generation—free spirits, free love, antiestablishment—Woodstock and all the rest. Mama played guitar and dabbled, but Daddy was a good painter. He was doing really well, with shows and sales and all, but then in my junior year at VCU, he was diagnosed with multiple sclerosis. Mama couldn't deal with it. She left him, and then she died when her van ran off a mountain on her way out to California to a folk festival."

"I'm sorry," was all he could think of to say. It was the most she'd said about herself in all the time he'd known her. He had an idea there was a lot more that was every bit as painful. The lady was nothing if not resilient. Tough as old boots, as she put it.

"What about you?" she said, her smile only slightly tremulous.

"What about me?"

"Well, I've told you the whole story of my life, so now it's your turn."

He was tempted to tell her, damned if he wasn't. Not that she'd believe him.

On the other hand, she just might. For a young widow who'd endured more than her share of the world's woes—some of it Cindy had revealed, the rest he'd only guessed at—she was far too gullible.

"Well now, where to start," he mused. "Shall I tell you about my parents? No, they're nowhere near as interesting as yours were. How about my great-grandfather, the moonshine magnate. Or about my cousin, the felon, or—"

"Be serious," she chided, laughing. She had an infectious laugh. He didn't think he would ever tire of hearing it.

"Right. Seriously, I grew up in Connecticut, lived in New York for the past fifteen or so years."

"What do you actually do?"

"You mean besides changing tires and planting tomatoes?"

"Whatever it is, if you aren't any better at it than you are at gardening and tire changing, you can't afford to buy my house."

They hadn't mentioned the sale recently. In an unspoken agreement, they'd postponed winding things up, even though there was no longer any reason to delay.

He'd already told her about his degrees, and that he was a retired businessman. "I was in electronics. Manufacturing, that is, not servicing."

She grinned that sassy grin of hers. "Now, that I can believe. I'm still not quite convinced you're not some kind of a spy, but I can't see any company hiring you to service anything."

"Gee, thanks for the vote of confidence."

"You're welcome. What about marriage? I mean, have you ever been?"

"Married? No."

"At your age, isn't that a little strange?"

"I don't know, is it? Maybe I never had time. Actually, I came close once—fairly recently."

"Who? I mean, what happened? No, I mean, I'm really sorry, Harrison. It's none of my business. You don't have to tell me if you don't want to, but why didn't it work out? I mean, I'm just curious, because if you want to know what I think, I think the woman must be crazy. For all your faults, you'd make a wonderful husband."

He didn't know whether to laugh or take umbrage. "All my faults, huh? Would you care to enumerate them?"

"No. Not really. Most of them are pretty minor, anyway. I've sort of gotten used to them by now."

"Then maybe you ought to snap me up before some other lucky woman puts in a bid."

"You're laughing at me, aren't you?"

"Would I do that?" he asked in mock disbelief.

"Absolutely. I didn't used to think you had a sense of humor, but you do. You're not as bossy as you used to be, either."

"That sounds encouraging."

"And you catch on fast. You're willing to learn, and you'd be surprised at how many men aren't. I mean, before you can learn something, first you have to be willing to admit you don't know it all. Some men would rather eat live bait."

The shadow was back in her eyes. She was thinking about Barnes again. If the bastard hadn't taken off in a drunken rage and driven into the side of a building, Harrison could have cheerfully wrung his neck.

But then, if Barnes hadn't died, neither of them would have been here now.

He knew about the wreck. The family had made a stab at damage control, but now that he was back on-line and had a clue as to what he was looking for, it had been easy enough to fill in the blanks.

"You were in the electronics business, weren't you? You could have said so."

"I thought I had."

"I'll bet you were part of management. No man could get that bossy working on an assembly line."

"Don't count on it, honey. Personality traits are as much genetic as acquired."

"I'm going to make sure Jimmy grows up in the right environment, with the right influences."

She didn't say it, but he knew what she was thinking. Between her folks and his old man, the kid had a pretty unreliable gene pool to draw from. She was going to have her work cut out for her, raising a boy in today's climate without a strong male role model at her side.

Thunder rumbled in the distance. Harrison became aware of the intensified scent of mud, river and forest. Swarms of mosquitoes came out of the woods. All at once, Cleo started slapping her arms and Harrison started swearing. They collided in the doorway, laughing, swatting, trying to escape the droning horde of insects.

Claiming exhaustion, she left him soon after that. Later, sprawled in the big leather-covered chair, Harrison stared unseeingly at the massive empty fireplace and thought about heat loss and hot dogs. Once when he happened to be home on the Fourth of July, rain had canceled the party at a friend's house. He'd asked if he could invite Timothy over and roast hot dogs in the fireplace.

His mother had told him not to be absurd. He'd ended up having lunch in the kitchen with the staff while his parents had gone to the club.

He seldom thought about his childhood, seeing no reason to dwell on what had not been a particularly memorable portion of his life. Nor did he now. Instead, he turned his thoughts to Cleo. By now, she'd have finished nursing Jimmy and doing all that nuzzling stuff new mothers did. At least, she did. He seriously doubted if his own mother ever had.

Cleo would be leaning over the crib, watching to see if Jimmy was going to go to sleep or fret awhile. Harrison knew the exact way her face would soften, her eyes would get that molten amber look, her lips would part. She'd touch the baby, maybe adjust the covers. She was an inveterate shoulder-patter, an arm-clasper, a hand-toucher. He couldn't count the number of times she'd done it to him. Nothing sexual about it. She simply didn't have her emotions under control yet. He'd even seen her squeeze Ada Davis's arm when the woman had stood beside her watching the baby sleep.

Come to think of it, he seldom missed a chance to touch Cleo, either. The casual brush in passing. Lifting her hair when it fell over her brow and her arms were full of Jimmy. Totally nonsexual. Even in the old days, he would never have considered having an affair with a woman like her.

Not that he was thinking about it now.

All right, so she was warm, lush, even desirable. She was far too impulsive, far too unsophisticated—far too unmanageable.

Hell, she'd even cried when Ada discovered that nest of mice and insisted on hauling them outside in a bucket. She'd been going to drown them, but Cleo had put her foot down.

"Mice invite snakes. You want to wake up one day and find the whole house full of rat snakes again? I'd almost sooner clean up after mice than after one o' them big old rat snakes. They splotch all over the floor. Hardest thing to scrub up is snake splotch."

Cleo had been teary but suitably chastened. Harrison had been amused at the time, but in this case, he was on Ada's side. No snakes. No mice. No varmints of any kind, and as soon as the deed to the house was in his name, that damned flea-bitten, wall-hung menagerie was out of here, too.

He heard the sound of a door opening and closing. By now she'd probably wandered into the bathroom, shedding her clothes along the way. She was not exactly the world's neatest person.

Neatness was important. No man could function efficiently amid chaos. To that end, he'd always had a small army working quietly behind the scenes, both at home and at work, to insure his orderly, serene way of life, leaving him free to devote his energies to far more important matters.

Although, come to think of it, he'd relaxed his standards a bit lately. Lately, he'd relaxed, period. Not only that, it had been weeks since he'd felt that old tightness at the back of his neck—the throbbing at his temple.

With a half-smoked cigar and a half-empty cup of coffee beside him, the latest edition of *Forbes* and an untidy stack of newspapers on the floor by his chair, he turned his mind to the past—to a way of life that was slipping further and further into the distance.

Expecting to feel the usual pain, the usual sense of

loss and frustration, he felt only a vague sense of release.

"God, what if it's communicable," he muttered. If he didn't watch himself, he'd be turning into a beach bum.

Cleo. Without even trying, the woman was starting to undermine a lifetime of hard-earned self-discipline.

Cleo... By now, she'd be stepping into the shower. Fine-tuning the mix. Reaching for the scented soap she used, which invariably triggered a whole range of erotic images. He pictured her soaping her body, head tipped back, eyes closed, water trailing over her breasts, her hips....

Snatching a paper off the top of the stack, he rustled through to the business section, scowling at the fine print. LLI was up two points since Monday. It had dropped six immediately after the buyout, recovered the loss and was courting record territory.

She slept in cotton, not silk. With her hair in a braid that was always coming apart by the time she woke up in the morning. He even knew what it looked like in the middle of the night, when she roused to nurse the baby.

"Get a grip, Lawless," he muttered. Standing, he stretched, tried to convince himself he was tired enough to sleep, and then swore softly. There was no way out. Either he sat up and thought about her, or he went to bed and dreamed about her. Neither option figured into his carefully made plans.

But then, what else in his life had worked out the way he'd planned it? Lately, too damned little.

Items one and two? He had trouble even remembering what they'd been. Somewhere around item three—or was it four?—things had completely fallen apart.

They ate dry cereal for breakfast the next day, with Jimmy fussing in the bassinet Harrison had driven all the way to Manteo to purchase.

"He'll outgrow it in no time." Cleo warned him again. She'd said the same thing when he'd first brought it inside.

"So? Save it for the next edition."

"There won't be any future editions."

"I wouldn't bet on that. You're a natural."

"I'll leave it here when I go."

It was the first time in weeks either of them had mentioned the inevitable parting. He added another spoonful of sugar to his already sweetened cereal and scowled. "Do that. It'll be a handy place to keep kindling for the fireplace."

"Marla might want to have another baby."

He looked up so quickly the sugar spoon missed the bowl, fell to the table and tumbled off onto the floor. "You want to run that one by me again?"

"That's why she came here, isn't it? To look the place over? Rip will love it. I'm not sure Marla will, but at least you can spend part of your time here. You can fly into Norfolk from anywhere in the world and drive down in only a couple of hours."

"And you call me bossy? Lady, I might be bossy, but at least I'm not trying to plan your life for you."

"You said you'd seriously considered marriage once. It was Marla, wasn't it?"

He felt around on the floor for the sugar spoon, brushed it off with his fingers and dropped it back into the bowl. Ada Davis's floors were clean enough to eat off. "I might have considered it at one time or another. Not recently, though."

"Then why did you invite her down here?"

"Did it ever occur to you that one of the reasons a man buys a place like this is so that he can invite his friends to visit?"

He knew he'd blundered before the words were even out of his mouth. "I'm sorry, Cleo. Another fault of mine you forgot to list is a total lack of tact."

"That's not a fault. If it is, it's only a minor one. But, Harrison, what went wrong? Was it because of me? My being here, I mean? If I'd thought about it in time, I would have explained to her, but what with the baby and all, it never even occurred to me until a few days ago that anyone would misunderstand. Maybe if I called and—"

"Forget it. Honey, I've known Marla for years."

Honey? Well, hell. When in Rome...

"We've had a—well, I guess you could call it a low-level involvement for some time, but there's been nothing between us other than friendship in more than a year."

"But you were hoping to start it up again, weren't you? Else you'd never have invited her down here before you'd even signed the final papers. I have a feeling she was hoping, too, until she got a look at the lodge. I don't think she liked it very much. Not that she said anything, but then, she's too well mannered to insult her host."

"Not to mention her hostess."

To his great delight, she blushed. Sounding flustered, she said, "I'm hardly that. Maybe next time—"

"There won't be a next time."

"Oh. Well—at least you have good taste in women. Better than some men I can think of."

He had to smile. "Oh, I don't know about that. If you're talking about Barnes, he showed excellent taste at least once, I can vouch for that."

Her smile was more rueful than amused. "If you mean what I think you mean, then thank you. That's one of the nicest things anyone's said to me in a long time."

After breakfast, Cleo scraped the leftovers from the previous night's dinner into a pan and took it out for the crows. As Jimmy was still awake, she banged on the pan with a spoon. Harrison teased her about her bird-feeding habits, but she liked watching the huge things collect, swooping from branch to branch, waiting for her to go inside. She would like to think someday they'd be tame and trusting enough to come while she was still outside.

Well, of course, that would never happen.

"You need a dog," Harrison said quietly from the other side of the screen door.

"Not many apartments allow dogs."

"I'm talking about now. Here."

"I won't be here much longer. Harrison, that's something we need to talk about. Do you have a few minutes?" Dusting the crumbs from her hands, she opened the door and then stepped back when he didn't move away.

With the morning light slanting down on his lean features, she found it almost impossible not to stare. If she'd brought her paints with her, she would have been tempted to do a portrait of him to take with her. To remember.

As if she could ever forget.

"I just heard another bulletin. Your friendly neighborhood convict's still on the loose."

"He'll be miles and miles away from here by now. Yesterday they were saying he'd been seen in Georgia."

"Last week he was reported in Virginia."

"So there, you see? Like I said, he's miles and miles from here."

"About that dog—"

"I'd rather talk about seeing Mrs. Dunn and signing whatever we have to sign so you can send for the rest of your things and start getting settled, and I can decide where I'm going to move and get started on that. I've given up on sending out any more résumés. Somebody, somewhere, is darned well going to hire me. I have a good feeling about it."

"A good feeling," he said, his face totally unreadable.

"A really good feeling," she emphasized, trying hard to shore up her crumbling resolve.

From the kitchen came the plaintive strains of a somebody-done-me-wrong song. From the woods came the sounds of the crows squabbling over bread crusts and the remains of last night's casserole.

"Close the screen door, you're letting in mosquitoes," Harrison said quietly.

She moved the necessary few inches for the screen door to shut. He didn't. She was so close she could smell the scent of his aftershave, see the faint dark mask of his freshly shaved beard. No power on earth could have prevented her from lifting her face. By the time his lips brushed hers, her eyes were closed tightly, shutting out all but the reality of his arms around her, his hard, warm body pressed against hers—the feel of two hearts gone wild.

The kiss was everything a kiss could be and more. Hungry. She was starved for the touch, the taste of him. Tender. It was that, too, in the way he held her, taking care not to crush her sensitive breasts too tightly against his chest.

Feelings rioted through her body. Half-formed thoughts tumbled about in her head, thoughts of what was happening and shouldn't be. Of how a thing could feel so inevitable and yet be so impossible.

He lifted his mouth and stared down at her, looking every bit as dazed as she felt. "This isn't—" he started to say.

"We can't—"

"I know, I know," he groaned.

He was fully aroused, there was no disguising it. No way either of them could pretend it hadn't happened to both of them. "I didn't know it was possible—I mean, it's been so long—it's too soon."

He nodded as if he knew exactly what she was trying to say. One of his hands sloped over her hips, holding her against him. She reacted instinctively, moving against him, aching for more.

He touched her hair, tugging out pins, fingering her braid until it tumbled down around her shoulders. "I've been wanting to do that since the first time I saw you," he whispered.

"You can't have. I was big as a cow. I was all puffy and ugly and cross."

"You were beautiful and frightened and I thought you were a complete flake."

"I was. I am. Oh, Harrison, this doesn't make any sense at all. We're nothing at all alike."

"It makes perfect sense to me. My timing might be a bit off, but that's nothing a little patience won't take care of."

Cleo forced herself to move out of his arms. Telling him no was probably the hardest thing she would ever have to do, and considering her past, that was saying a lot.

But then, her past was precisely the reason why she had to say it now, while she still had the willpower. Backgrounds counted. Where a person came from, how they were raised had a lot to do with who they were and what they expected from life.

She had loved the wrong kind of man once and lived to regret it. She and Niles had come from totally different backgrounds. It had been a disastrous match. She was just now recovering her feeling of self-worth. For the sake of her son, she couldn't afford to risk losing it again.

He was a highfalutin Northerner, for heaven's sake! At least Southerners, regardless of social status, had certain references in common, yet even that hadn't helped with the Barneses.

She opened her mouth to speak, but he laid a finger over her lips. "Shh, don't say anything now. But think about it, will you?"

Think about what?

As if she didn't know.

As if she could help herself.

Hearing Ada's firm step on the wide pine floor,

they moved farther apart. Cleo felt shaky—hot and cold at the same time, as if she were coming down with something.

"Comp'ny coming!" the housekeeper sang out.

"Oh hell, not again," Harrison muttered.

"My sentiments exactly." But secretly she was glad of anything to dilute the tension between them.

Twelve

Even covered with dust, there was no mistaking the late-model Seville. Cleo felt her shoulders begin to sag. Forcefully, she squared them and stepped out onto the front deck. Thankful for the steady strength of the man behind her, she murmured, "It's Niles's parents."

"I take it you're not too thrilled to see them."

"No, but I'm not surprised, either. I wrote and told them about Jimmy, but they'd have found out, anyway. Henry has...ways of knowing things. Things he wants to know, at least."

Henry Barnes had lost weight, but he was still far more formidable than any short, paunchy, red-faced man had a right to be. "Where is he? Where's my grandson?"

"Hello, Father Barnes, Mother Barnes."

Cleo wondered, not for the first time, how it was possible to be intimidated by a woman wearing pearls, sensible shoes, an ugly hat and a shapeless flowered dress. It had to be Vesper's attitude, that inborn assumption of superiority that she was far too refined to mention.

"Where is Niles's son?" Henry Barnes demanded.

"Jimmy's asleep. Would you like to look in on him?"

For a single moment, Vesper looked almost as if she were wavering on the verge of thawing. Hastily, Cleo made the introductions. "Mother Barnes, Father Barnes, this is Harrison Lawless, my…houseguest."

Vesper's lips thinned disapprovingly. Henry's small eyes narrowed. It was Henry who pronounced their joint disapproval in two words. "I *see*."

Cleo didn't ask what he thought he saw. Didn't have to. She opened her mouth to explain that Harrison was in the process of buying the lodge and then snapped it shut again. She didn't owe them an explanation. Didn't owe them a darned thing. She'd been under no obligation to tell them about the baby, but she'd written, anyway, knowing they'd probably act as if they had a greater right to her baby than she did.

We'll just see about that, she thought grimly.

Ada Davis chose that moment to elbow through the front door with a tray of iced tea. Four glasses, tinkling with ice cubes, irresistible when both the temperature and the humidity hovered somewhere in the low nineties.

"Let's go inside where it's cool. Mother Barnes, would you like to—"

"I'd like to see my grandson. That's why we're here. I believe Henry has a few things to say to you if your *houseguest* will allow us a moment of privacy." Vesper's head wagged self-righteously at the word *houseguest*. White purse clutched in her white-gloved hands, she picked her way across the freshly swept deck as if it were a chicken yard and she were wearing house slippers. In all of five years, the only time Cleo had ever seen the woman looking less than flawlessly groomed had been the night Niles was killed. She'd aged since then, but some things hadn't changed. She would go to her grave wearing hat, gloves, stockings and corset, a circle of rouge on each dry, withered cheek.

Harrison held the door and Ada followed the two women inside, still holding the tea tray. Henry paused just inside the door and favored Harrison with another of his speculative looks. "Lawless, hmm? From around here? I understand the name was once known in the area."

"According to old records, I believe it was fairly well-known," Harrison allowed.

"Hmm. Have we met before?"

"I don't believe we have. I'm sure I'd have remembered."

"Hmm."

"I demand to see my grandson," Vesper Barnes announced, wattles trembling self-righteously.

Cleo started to respond, but Harrison beat her to the punch. "Shall I bring him out? I'd better change him first." He'd held the boy a number of times, even changed his diaper once or twice. The first few times he'd been scared stiff, but he was getting the hang of it. Infants, he'd discovered, for all they were greedy, uncivilized little hedonists, had a way of slipping under a man's guard.

Right on cue, Vesper began to huff. "Well, I never."

Henry said, "Now, see here, young man—"

Ada plopped the tray down on the coffee table, saying, "I'll change him and bring him out. Better'n having him wake up in a room full of strangers."

"I'm sorry, I forgot—Ada, these are Jimmy's

grandparents, Mr. and Mrs. Barnes. Mother B, Father B, this is our friend and housekeeper, Mrs. Davis.''

"*Our* housekeeper? Would you mind telling me just what is going on here, Cleopatra?''

Harrison nearly strangled on his tea. The woman was a walking, talking stereotype. "Cleopatra? You want to explain, or shall I?'' he taunted softly, gray eyes gleaming with wicked amusement.

Cleo shot him a stern look. Evidently she failed to appreciate the humorous aspects of the situation. She was holding up pretty well, but he could tell she was weakening. Damned good thing he was here to protect her interests. He wouldn't put it past these two overstuffed vultures to whip out an agreement, force her to sign the thing and then drive off with her baby, leaving her to grieve herself to death.

No way. Not on his watch.

"Thank you, Mrs. Davis,'' he said as Ada marched out of the room. He turned back to the elderly couple. It hadn't taken him long to size them up. Barnes was easy. Ambitious, pretentious, more than willing to cut corners as long as he could get away with it. His wife was straight as a stick, but maybe not quite all she pretended to be. He'd lay odds her lineage wouldn't bear too close scrutiny.

But then, that pretty well summed up his own background, he thought, amused. "You're probably wondering what I'm doing here. I'm thinking of buying Cleo's house when and if she decides to sell. We're still discussing terms.''

Mrs. Barnes looked suspiciously from one to the other, almost as if she expected them to fall to the floor and start tearing away each other's clothing.

Damned if he wasn't tempted to oblige.

Henry, however, was off on another tack. "Lawless. Don't tell me, don't tell me. *Forbes* magazine, January issue, right? That semiconductor thing. The merger. My God, you're not *that* Lawless, are you? Vesper, shut up a minute, will you?"

Vesper was rattling on about housekeepers, appearances and the importance of early enrollment in the proper school. Cleo was uncomfortable. That panicky look was back in her eyes. Any minute now she was going to come out with one of her off-the-wall remarks and blow things wide open.

Harrison glanced uneasily at Henry Barnes, who was gaping like a beached fish. When Vesper said, "Niles was always a good student," he took the opportunity to deflect the man's attention.

"I'm sure he was, Mrs. Barnes. Jimmy's already showing signs of advanced intelligence." How intelligent did a five-week-old baby need to be to process milk? At least he did it efficiently, Harrison could personally vouch for that.

"Vesper, for God's sake, shut up! Do you know who this man is? Do you have the slightest idea who our Cleo's been keeping company with?"

"*Our* Cleo?" both Harrison and Cleo echoed.

Harrison thought, *Their* Cleo? When hell froze over.

It was left to Cleo to say, "I'm not keeping company with anyone, and if I were, it's nobody's business but mine, but thank you for your concern."

"Henry, do something. I'll not have Niles's baby exposed to—"

"Here he is, folks, clean drawers and all. Grandmaw, you want to hold him a minute before he starts kicking up a fuss for his breakfast? It don't take him long once he wakes up.'' A beaming Ada presented the small bundle as if he were the crown jewels on a satin cushion.

''Oh my goodness,'' Vesper murmured, twisting her head sideways to peer down at the tiny face. ''Wait a minute...'' She peeled off her gloves, tossed them aside, then held out her arms. ''Oh, you precious thing. Henry, he looks just like Niles did at that age. Henry, look, doesn't he look like Niles? Oh, my blessed land, would you look at those eyes. They're the exact same shade of blue.''

Harrison watched as the woman, who could probably flash-freeze an upstart with a single glance, morphed into a doting grandmother. He watched Jimmy's slightly cockeyed gaze try to focus on the unfamiliar face.

And then he turned his attention to Cleo, cataloging the array of emotions flickering across her mobile features. Surprise. Relief. Guilt—and something almost like fear.

And sympathy?

Yeah, sympathy. Now, why didn't that surprise him? For a woman who'd managed to survive five years with this pair of piranhas, not to mention the abusive bastard she'd been married to, she was still far too soft for her own good.

Barnes was staring at him with a look of increasing awe. Harrison recognized the symptoms. Ever since he'd let himself be talked into giving that interview to *Prominence Magazine,* he'd been fawned over by people who ought to know better. As if what he'd managed to accomplish somehow set him apart from the rest of humanity.

He had a feeling Cleo was about to get an earful before he could put things into perspective. He should have explained before now, only he was afraid it might change their relationship.

Hell, he didn't even know what their relationship was.

He knew what he wanted it to be, though.

The Barneses stayed for lunch and then stayed for an early dinner. Cleo reluctantly offered to make up the south wing for them. Vesper said yes, please. She'd lost a lot of her starch in the process of getting acquainted with her grandson.

Henry overruled her, but then, that was nothing new. Now that she'd been away from them for a while, the pecking order was obvious. Living under their roof, Cleo had been aware only of the constant flow of criticism directed her way. First there was the way she dressed and the way she spoke. Next, the friends she chose and the books she read, not to mention the worthy clubs she refused to join.

When Henry was home, there wasn't a single doubt as to just who ruled the roost. The minute he left for the office, Vesper took over. Her style was different, but she was every bit as ruthless.

Niles had been no help at all. Working for his father by day, dealing with his mother at night, he had various ways of boosting his own battered ego, none of them very pleasant.

God, she wished they'd go! Henry was obviously dying to linger, but she heard him tell Harrison they were the guests of close friends at their cottage in Duck.

"Cottage, ha! Place cost a cool million if it cost a dime, but Tom likes to call it his little beach cottage." Henry went on to mention the name of a congressman who was under indictment on a number of charges concerning money laundering and fraud.

"I'm considering representing the man. Bad business—don't believe a word of it myself. All the same, it's going to be a big suit, plenty of publicity, big settlement. Did I happen to mention I'm being urged to run for office in the next election?" His expression was a masterpiece of coy self-deprecation. "But then, campaigns take money, even with reforms. Still, there are ways and means, am I right?" He removed his glasses, polished them and replaced them on his florid face. "Yessir, ways and means, but then, what's good for politics is good for business and vice versa, I always say. Tit for tat."

Cleo could almost find it in her heart to feel sorry for the man she'd once hated with a passion. He was pathetic. More despicable than hateful. Poor Niles. Poor Vesper.

She watched the interaction between the two men, not at all surprised to see Harrison take quiet control of the conversation.

Henry mentioned a certain stock deal. Harrison glanced at his watch.

Henry said, "I could get you in on this. A phone call to my broker—no trouble, glad to do it."

Harrison smiled with his lips, not his eyes, and said, "Mr. Barnes—"

"Henry. My friends call me Henry."

"Henry, I believe I'll pass, but thanks anyway."

"Now, son, you don't want to do that. As it happens, I have inside information—"

Harrison glanced at Cleo with growing respect. To think she'd lived in their cave and survived. With a little more savoir faire and a different accent, he thought, the man could have been his own father. Feeling the old familiar tension begin to gather at the back of his neck, he flexed his hands, willing himself to relax. This poor jerk wasn't worth another coronary.

He glanced at Cleo again and let his gaze linger, appreciating the way the light played over the side of her face. It reminded him of the watercolor of the reading woman hanging on his bedroom wall. What was the reader reading? What was she thinking?

What was Cleo thinking? So far he'd managed to direct the conversation away from the danger zone, but he had a feeling something was going to hit the fan as soon as the Barneses left.

Finally, holding the drowsy baby in her arms, Cleo went out onto the deck to see her in-laws on their way. It was nearly nine o'clock, but not quite dark.

Harrison braced himself, but she came inside and settled into the rocking chair without saying a word. He told himself he'd been worrying over nothing. She obviously hadn't been listening to Barnes, she'd been too busy standing guard to see that Granny didn't abduct her baby.

Cleo rocked Jimmy and ignored Harrison. When the silence began to eat at his nerves, he said, "I think they both took it pretty well, don't you? I'm surprised Henry didn't show more interest."

"Mmm-hmm." She began to hum with no regard at all for the melody.

"Jimmy was at his best."

"Jimmy's always at his best."

"But his best," Harrison observed, "would be even better if he could figure out the difference between night and day."

"There's nothing wrong with being a night person."

"A night person. Right." He gave up. Maybe she hadn't caught on to the fact that Barnes had been hinting around for a backer. That on recognizing him, he'd done everything but genuflect. That her father-in-law was a petty sycophant, and that Harrison was slightly more than a retired businessman.

Or maybe he was just that. Oh hell, he didn't know who he was anymore, much less who he was trying to become. Next time he picked a midlife crisis, he might just try out for a motorcycle gang.

Distracted by a vision of lamplight on soft skin, of hollows beneath flawlessly sculpted cheekbones, Harrison waited in growing frustration. It was the single emotion he'd never learned to handle successfully. Probably because he'd seldom been forced to handle it. He'd had staff for that.

"So?" he said finally.

"So what?"

He wondered if she was being flippant. "So what do you think? Anything in particular on your mind?"

"About the visit? Not really. Vesper said they're going back to Richmond tomorrow."

Harrison shook his head slowly. One of them

wasn't connecting the right dots. "She'll be back. I give her a week."

"Jimmy and I won't be here."

Tension slammed back full force. "What do you mean, you won't be here?"

"For heaven's sake, what's wrong with you tonight?"

"Nothing's wrong with me! What do you expect when you come out with a crackpot announcement like that?"

"Crackpot? And I didn't *announce* anything. I've never made any secret of my plans."

"Don't try to wiggle out of it. You weren't in any great hurry to leave before, so what's changed? Are you afraid Granny's going to bring reinforcements next time? What about this Holmes fellow? Is he friend or foe?"

"Holmes?" she asked. "Ooh…you must have been listening in on my phone messages. He's neither. Pierce tried to find me, but it had nothing to do with Henry or Vesper. He and Cindy are now involved. They wanted the deed to the house, that's all. Cindy assured me they weren't interested in me or Jimmy."

"And you believe her?"

"Cindy has little reason to lie to me. Yes, I believe her."

"Great. Then why run away?"

"I'm not running away. I always planned to leave once we closed on the house, you know that."

"Don't hand me that. You've been blowing hot and cold about giving up this place ever since I talked you into selling it."

"You didn't talk me into anything. I just—needed a little more time to think things through."

Harrison slowly shook his head. "Lady, you are a piece of work."

"Shh, don't wake up Jimmy. I'm going to put him down, and then if you want to talk about it, we'll talk about it, but I won't change my mind."

Witchery, he thought, watching her walk away. She'd kicked off her shoes. She had anklebones again. Nice ankles. Superb ankles. Underneath that slow, sexy smile and that slow, husky drawl, the woman was either sharp as a pawnbroker or a genuine, certified flake. Damned if he could figure out which, and the scariest part was, he no longer cared.

Waiting for her to return, he got up and started pacing, and then he started swearing. So much for his new stress-free life-style. He'd set out with a plan, a backup plan and a contingency plan. He hadn't got where he was without learning the importance of careful planning.

The trouble was, not a single one of his plans had worked out. And if that wasn't hard enough to swallow, there was the fact that he no longer gave a damn. Somewhere along the line, his priorities had changed radically. He wasn't sure just when, much less how, but he knew precisely where to lay the blame.

So the woman was sexy. Even pregnant she'd been sexy. So he was finding it impossible to keep his hands off her. That didn't mean...

Yeah, it did mean. It meant exactly what he was afraid it meant. That now, instead of being addicted to the adrenaline high that came from the fierce cut and thrust of the business world, he was addicted to a woman.

And not just any woman. This one wasn't going to fit neatly into one of his careful plans. In the first place, she was an artist. Everybody knew artists and engineers didn't mix. Hell, he wasn't even sure they spoke the same language.

He knew now who had painted those watercolors. Even if he hadn't finally made out the signature, he'd have figured it out, because they were just like her. All muted, flowing colors, hazy, merging images, with hints of something just beyond the line of sight. Taken literally, not a one of them made sense.

Taken literally, neither did she half the time. And yet, the paintings spoke to him the same way she did. Both were light on structure, heavy on substance, the sum greater than the parts.

His life had been about structure. Seldom, if ever, had he given a single thought to substance. He'd been founder, CEO and chief stockholder of an international corporation. What more substance did a man need?

The titles no longer applied. What remained? What if she looked inside him and saw only emptiness? His money wasn't going to impress her. The fact that he was considered one of the world's most eligible bachelors wasn't going to matter a hill of beans. He could plead poor health and throw himself on her mercy, but he'd rather die than see pity in her eyes.

The plain truth was, he didn't know how to deal with a woman like Cleo. Hell, she even knew more about cars than he did.

He wandered outside, waiting for her to finish nursing, changing and bedding down the baby for the night. Or at least the next couple of hours. After a while a soft drizzle began to fall. He stood on the deck, letting the rain soak his hair, plaster his shirt to his body. It made about as much sense as anything else he'd done recently.

Ada Davis came outside and raised her umbrella. "Need a good rain. Garden's dry as a bone."

He murmured an agreement. If she'd said the house was on fire, he'd have had the same reaction, which was no reaction at all.

"If you're waiting for Cleo to join you, she's holed up in her bedroom with yesterday's paper, going over them help wanted ads. I told her she was going to ruin her eyes, reading in bed like that."

"Help wanted— Thanks, Mrs. Davis. I'd better get in out of the rain."

She shook her head, muttered something about some folks and hurried out to her truck. Soaked to the skin, Harrison took time to shower and change, and then he made cocoa and sandwiches. As a peace offering, it wasn't much, but then, it wasn't peace he was after, it was a showdown.

Standing just outside her door, he balanced the tray and took a deep, bracing breath. He was no good at this. Management problems he could deal with. If he had to. He'd seldom had to, because his was a well-run organization. He'd dealt successfully with mergers and buyouts and thwarted a few attempted hostile takeovers. What he was about to do now was scary as hell. Mainly because he wasn't certain of his goal, much less how to achieve it. Much less what he was going to do when he succeeded.

That he would fail never entered his mind.

He rapped lightly. "Hey, open up. I know you're awake in there."

"It's late. Go away, Harrison."

"I've got hot cocoa," he called softly through the door.

"Cocoa and what?"

"Peanut-butter-and-jelly sandwiches."

"What kind?"

So far so good. She'd taken the bait. "Chunky and fig, respectively," he called through the door.

By the time she opened the door, his confidence was soaring. "Oh, for goodness' sake, come in before you wake the whole household."

Trying not to look too much like a well-fed tiger, he followed her inside. As the household consisted of two adults and one sleeping infant, he thought he could handle it.

A few minutes later, he wasn't so sure.

Thirteen

Not even the scent of peanut butter and scorched cocoa could defuse the tension as Cleo stepped back to allow Harrison to set the tray on her dresser. The very air seemed to tremble.

This was a mistake.

A bigger mistake had been leaving him out on the deck without settling matters between them once and for all.

The biggest mistake of all had been letting him in her house that very first day, when she'd opened her door to see a stranger with cool gray eyes, a beard-shadowed jaw that was aggressively square, his fist lifted to knock again.

No it hadn't. Her worst mistake had been falling in love with another control freak. The only difference was, Harrison was strong where Niles had been weak. Harrison did his controlling—or tried to—in the nicest possible way.

Nor had Harrison made any effort to sweep her off her feet, the way Niles had done. But then, Niles had had another bride all picked out for him and needed a foolproof excuse not to marry her.

Cleo had been that excuse, and she'd paid the price for it.

"Is he asleep?" Harrison's low-pitched voice undermined her determination with no effort at all. She nodded, tightening her robe, wishing she hadn't undressed. Wishing she'd pretended to be asleep. Wishing all sorts of things she had no business wishing.

"I was waiting for you to come back. We were going to talk, remember?" Leaning against the oak highboy, his legs crossed at the ankles, he could easily have been a male model—one of those sexy, classy, older men who wore sexy, classy, understated casuals and made every other man in the world look like an overdressed juvenile by comparison.

He'd been in her room countless times before. He'd brought her warm milk when she'd wakened in the night to nurse Jimmy, and stayed on to keep her company.

He'd nailed up shelves for Jimmy's treasures. He'd rocked in her rocking chair and read to her from the Sunday papers while she lay in bed with Jimmy sleeping beside her. Read her pieces on gardening and on child rearing, when she knew very well he was dying to turn to the business section.

Tonight he'd brought cocoa and PBJ sandwiches. So why did that serving tray remind her so much of a Trojan horse?

"Now, what was this about leaving?"

"It's time. Jimmy will be six weeks old next week." Did he know the significance of that? Probably not.

"You don't have to rush off," he said, and she laughed.

"I'd hardly call it rushing. But the lodge is yours if you still want it. I—I appreciate your patience."

"Dammit, it's not patience! You love this place. Why are you so eager to get rid of it?"

She threw up her hands. "I can't believe I'm hearing this. Look, we've had this discussion before. I like it here, but even if it were closer to town and I could find work in the area, it's too big, too isolated, and besides, I need the money."

She'd switched on her bedside lamp, determined to find something—a single lead, a direction. A goal. Instead, all she could think of was what she'd be leaving behind. "If you're offering me more time, Harrison, then thanks, but it won't work." Unless he was offering the rest of his life, time wasn't what she wanted from him.

Silence lay like a seductive pool between them, deep and calm, rife with hidden dangers. She tightened the sash of her robe and then loosened it again, conscious of the way she must look. Her waist still wasn't back down to its old measurement. Her breasts felt as if they weighed a ton. She'd never felt less desirable in her life, and never regretted it more.

"Cleo?"

"Oh, for heaven's sake, if you want the house, then tell Mrs. Dunn. If you've changed your mind, and I certainly couldn't blame you, then I'll just wait for another offer. But stop looking at me that way," she snapped.

"I like to look at you. I'd like to do more than—"

"You said you wanted to talk? Then say what you came to say and leave. It's late. I need to get some sleep before Jimmy wakes up and wants to nurse again."

Her breasts throbbed, and it wasn't from thinking

about Jimmy, it was because of the way he was looking at them. At her. As if he'd never seen a woman's
breasts before.

The first time he'd barged into the room when she
was nursing, they'd both been embarrassed. He'd
blushed and backed out, and for days after that, she
couldn't look at him without remembering the expression on his face.

The next time, too, had been accidental. They'd
both pretended a nonchalance neither of them had really felt, but after that he'd seemed to find one excuse
after another to join her while she nursed. He seemed
to take such pleasure in the small ritual that she'd let
him stay. Besides, she'd liked the feeling it gave her,
as if they were sharing something special.

After a while it had come to be a habit. The late-
night feedings. The snacks he'd brought, which
they'd shared once Jimmy fell asleep. She'd read
about new mothers looking forward to the time when
their babies slept the night through.

She wasn't one of them.

"Where will you go? What kind of job are you
looking for?"

"One with benefits, including an on-site nursery.
One I'm qualified for, which sort of limits the possibilities," she told him with a rueful smile. "Without
a degree, I can't teach. I'd make a good gallery manager—I can do everything from hang shows to keep
books. Show hanging is an art in itself. But the benefits, even if I could find an opening, are lousy."

"Ever think about marketing your work?"

She looked away. "It wouldn't sell. Some of the

best watercolorists I know can't make a living at it. Besides, mine's too…personal.''

He looked as if he were going to say something else but changed his mind. ''The Barneses would take you in.''

''Thanks, but they took me in once before, and I swore I'd never be taken in again. I know Vesper. She'd start out wanting to take Jimmy around and show him off to her friends. Next she'd tell me I looked tired. Then she'd hire a nanny, and next thing you know, she'd have him enrolled in Niles's old schools, all the way to choosing his university—and probably his major. No, Henry would choose that. Law.'' If she sounded bitter, it was because she felt bitter. And defensive. And vulnerable on far too many fronts.

''She lost her only son.''

''And I lost my only husband, so stop trying to make me feel guilty! Even if you're right and she's not trying to take him away from me, I can't let her and Henry do to Jimmy what they did to Niles. I'd sooner pitch a tent in Monroe Park than move back into that house and allow them to raise my son.''

At a sound from the sheet-draped crib, they both turned. Harrison quietly crossed the room to gaze down at the sleeping infant. With a sigh, Cleo joined him.

Jimmy smacked his lips in his sleep. His little knees were bent, his tiny hands flung over his head. His head was perfectly shaped now, but he was still bald as a gourd.

''He's just so beautiful,'' she whispered.

It seemed the most natural thing in the world when

Harrison slipped his arm around her waist. She let her head rest on his shoulder. Because she was tired, she told herself. Because her head was beginning to ache from a wearing day and too many unanswered questions.

"Tired?" he whispered.

She nodded.

"Your head hurts, doesn't it?"

"How did you know?"

"That little pucker between your eyebrows. Your eyes are darker when you're hurting."

"You see far too much," she said dryly.

"I see why you don't want to move back with your in-laws. What I don't see is why you can't stay on here."

Pulling away from his side, she dropped down onto the foot of the bed and pressed both hands against her temples. "Harrison, I can't go on drifting forever. I know you think I'm a—a flake. I'm not. Honestly, I'm as practical as a doormat, but—"

"Interesting choice of words."

"Don't go looking for hidden meanings. I've got things under control, I really have." The way a meteorologist had the weather under control. Watch what happens and then report on it.

The mattress sagged as he sat down beside her. She tilted toward him, struggled to resist the temptation to stay there and tried to think of something sensible to say. About the job market. The stock market. The hog market, for goodness' sake!

Lifting his hands, he slipped his fingers under hers and began to massage her temples while his thumbs circled gently over her cheekbones. Magically, the pain began to ebb.

She sighed. "That helps."

"I used to have a lot of headaches," he murmured. "Haven't had one in ages."

Who had massaged away his headaches? Marla? A streak of jealousy shot through her.

"Lean forward so I can get to the back of your neck. We'll ease the tension."

Wrong. In case he wasn't aware of it, the tension had tripled in the past two minutes.

He toppled her forward so that her forehead rested on his shoulder. His strong, incredibly comforting hands continued their steady pressure. "Better?" he murmured.

"Mmm-hmm."

Outside, the rain continued to beat down, emphasizing the seductive intimacy of the softly lighted room. His hands worked their way down her spine, stroking, pressing, easing tension. Creating tension of an entirely different sort.

Cleo thought, This isn't smart. I know exactly where this kind of thing can lead. And, oh Lord, I wish it would!

Dredging up her practical side, she said, "By the way, why was Henry so impressed? He seemed to think he knew you from somewhere."

"Shh, don't tense up again. How's your headache now?"

"Better. Almost gone, in fact." She wanted to take back the words in case he stopped doing what he was doing. Honesty fought a battle with sensuality and lost. "Hmm, yes—right there. That feels so-o-o good."

His thumbs worked their way up her spine. If this was supposed to be an exercise in relaxation, it wasn't working. *Earth to Cleo—wake up, you silly pigeon!* "What was I saying?" she murmured.

"Were you saying something?" His hands eased down her back, around her sides until the tips of his fingers brushed against her breasts. He was breathing through his mouth. Audibly. Rapidly.

"Oh, yes—about Henry." Anything to take her mind off what was happening to her. "The only thing that impresses Henry is money or power. I know you're not poor. Are you very rich, or maybe powerful? Poor Henry was practically groveling."

His hands grew still. Cleo told herself she was glad and tried to believe it, but he didn't remove his arms, and she didn't pull away.

"Would it make a difference if I were?"

"To Henry? You heard the way he was dropping the names of all those politicians. If you are—rich and famous, I mean—then he's probably dropping your name right this very..." His hands began to move again. "Ooh, right there. Yes, like that." She snuggled closer to allow him better access to all the places that ached for his touch.

Well, perhaps not *all* the places....

"Forget Henry," he said, his voice low, rough, almost unrecognizable. "Would it make a difference to you?"

His hands stopped moving again, and she sighed, realizing she was practically sitting in his lap. Reluctantly, she attempted to move away.

He refused to let her go. "Answer my question, Cleo. Would it make a difference if you knew I could afford to support you and Jimmy so that you wouldn't have to work at all?"

"Harrison, I'm hardly stupid. That car you drive didn't come in a box of Cracker Jacks. You're paying me five hundred dollars a week, which is way too much, and—"

"And you have yet to cash a single check."

"Because I haven't needed to! You keep feeding me! You've practically bought out every furniture store in two counties, and you haven't even moved in yet, at least not officially. I have a feeling you don't just work for that electronics company you mentioned, you probably own it."

"I did. Not anymore."

"You lost it? You lost everything, and that's why you're down here trying to start over?" Did he hesitate, or was it only her imagination?

"It's one of the reasons."

"Another one being?"

"Maybe I found something down here I value more than anything I left behind."

"Did you?" She held her breath. It was crazy to hope. Crazy to feel what she was feeling. Crazy to think he might be feeling it, too. Now that she finally had her hormones back under control, she refused to allow them to run her life again.

He was going to kiss her. She licked her lips nervously and waited. Carefully, he lowered her onto the bed, never once breaking contact with her eyes. The kiss began slowly, almost tentatively. She lifted her arms around his neck, and he groaned, and then he was lying half on top of her, his weight almost painful on her full breasts, but not nearly as painful as the ache his kiss—his tongue—his hands—triggered deep inside her.

Somehow, her robe fell open to her waist. Somehow, his shirt came unbuttoned. Cleo had seen his chest before. Now she explored to her heart's content, from the patch of hair in the center to the tiny tufts surrounding his nipples to the narrow streak that trailed downward to disappear under his belt. She traced the course and was tugging at his belt when he covered her hand with his.

"It's probably too soon," he whispered hoarsely, holding her hand, dragging his lips to her throat, where a throbbing pulse echoed the wild beat of her heart.

"No, it's not."

"I wouldn't want to—"

"I need—"

Broken sentences, broken promises, broken hearts. She'd been down this road before. It led nowhere, and yet...

His hands cupped her breasts so tenderly, relieving the weight. He kissed the blue-veined slopes and she wanted to tear off her wretched old nursing bra and bare herself to his kisses. Of all the deplorably, embarrassingly unsexy things she might have been wearing, it would have to be a heavy-duty, flannel-lined, snap-open nursing bra.

And she had stretch marks. And flab. She had never in her life wanted to be more desirable to a man and never felt less desirable. She should have known better.

"Wait," she whispered, "let me turn out the light." She reached for the lamp, but he caught her hand and brought it to his lips.

Harrison's heart was thundering. He was scared, but not too scared to notice that not even fear had a dampening effect on his fierce arousal. He reminded himself he was no longer the man he'd once been. With his genetic history, he couldn't—shouldn't—be doing this. What if he died in the act? It would be awful for her.

In spite of the doctor's assurances that there was no real reason why he shouldn't resume his sexual life, he kept thinking about all the stories he'd heard about men who'd died in their lovers' beds. Sometimes it was a mistress, sometimes only a one-night stand. It occurred to him that he'd never heard of a case where a man died in the arms of his wife after sex, which might indicate that guilt was a factor.

There was no guilt involved here. He wasn't sure just what was involved, which was one more reason for caution. He knew one thing: he'd never come close to feeling this way about Marla, or any other woman he'd ever slept with. How the devil was he supposed to control his emotions when he couldn't even understand them?

They lay there, his face in the curve of her shoulder, his arm resting across her waist. She smelled of soap, talcum and warm, aroused woman. It was all he could do not to risk it and let nature take its course. There were worse ways to die.

For her sake, he couldn't do it. She'd blame herself, and guilt was a hell of a legacy. She deserved better.

"Harrison?" she murmured. "I'm sorry."

He lifted his head, focusing on the face mere inches from his own. She looked flushed, damp, puzzled. "No, I'm the one who's sorry. I didn't tell you everything. I guess I didn't want you to think I was a complete crock."

"It's been almost six weeks." She watched him, her gaze moving over his face.

"Cleo, did you hear me? Honey, I let you down, and I'm sorry. I shouldn't have started anything like this. I only meant to talk things through so we knew where we stood."

She laughed, but there was no joy in it. "I guess now we know."

"We do?"

"Well, I know one thing—a nursing mother carrying about ten pounds of flab is not very seductive."

He swore softly and lifted his head so that he could look down into her face. "You can't believe that. Honey, I've never wanted any woman as much as I want you right now. If you need proof..."

When she went on looking up at him, it slowly dawned on him that she wasn't blaming him, she was blaming herself. "Ah, no, Cleo. You've got it all wrong." He had a feeling Barnes had played hell with her ego, but surely she knew how he felt about her. The proof was damned hard to conceal.

"You don't believe me?"

Silence. Could her self-confidence still be that fragile?

There was one way to convince her, and recklessly, he took it. Covering her hand with his, he guided her to the only hard evidence he could offer.

Her eyes widened. He shut his. When her fingers

closed convulsively around him, he nearly died. Heart pounding in his chest, he waited for the crushing pain. It didn't come.

"Then why...?" she whispered.

"You're not ready," he managed to say. "Are you?"

"Not quite—near enough."

"I don't have any protection."

"They say nursing mothers hardly ever conceive, at least not right at first."

He bit the bullet. For her, he could do no less. "Cleo, I've had a coronary."

He waited.

"So?"

Her hand was still on him, which was probably just as dangerous as if he were inside her, only he couldn't think of a way to remove it without increasing the risk of making her feel unwanted.

Unwanted! That was a laugh!

Against his will, he began to move his hips. Not much, but enough so that he knew he had to get out before he embarrassed himself at best and killed himself at worst.

He reached down and covered her hand with his, fully intending to remove it. Instead, he found himself guiding her, unable to resist the mindless drive to completion.

"I...can't...do...this," he rasped.

"Let me help you. Let me give you this much, at least."

And she did. Lord help him, she did. Explosively, embarrassingly, he came to her touch and cried out, something he had never before done.

Eventually, when he could catch his breath, he tried to frame an apology. She whispered something, but the words were lost when Jimmy, startled out of his sleep, began to wail.

He thought she said, "Wait," but he didn't hang around to find out. When the door shut behind him, he was clutching his shirt, clutching his pants, wondering how far he'd have to drive to outrun his embarrassment. Alaska sounded like a good place to start.

Breakfast was awful. It was Saturday. Ada didn't come on Saturdays. There was only Jimmy and Cleo and Harrison, and nothing to dilute the awkwardness.

"Coffee?" he asked. "You haven't had any yet."

He felt his face burning and hoped she didn't pick up on the double entendre. It was purely unintentional.

"I'm not hungry."

"It's the weather."

It wasn't the weather, and they both knew it. It was the knowledge that he had come apart in her hands last night, had screamed out his pleasure, waking the baby, and then left her to deal with the crying boy while Harrison slunk away to shower and spend the rest of the night brooding.

At least, he'd expected to brood. Much to his surprise, he'd fallen asleep and hadn't roused until the birds tuned up outside his window.

"My father died at the age of forty-seven of a massive heart attack." Cleo's habit of uttering non sequiturs was rubbing off on him.

"I'm sorry, Harrison. Mine was two years older

than that when he died. I told you he had MS, didn't
I?''

"You don't understand what I'm trying to tell you,
do you?''

She nodded and stirred her untouched cereal.
"You're afraid of dying.''

"Well…hell. Wouldn't you be?'' He didn't know
how she did it, but she managed to make him feel
like a kid trying to avoid a shot in the doctor's office.

"Did what we did last night cause any—you know,
problems?''

"You mean, other than terminal embarrassment?''

She reacted to the wry touch of humor with one of
those slow, sweet, sexy smiles that never failed to
play havoc with his brain.

Not to mention a few more body parts.

"You think you were embarrassed?'' She chuckled, and the husky sound streaked through him like
lightning. "What about me? Acres of flab, a heavy
cotton harness designed to keep me from leaking. If
you think any woman feels desirable under those conditions, you're flat-out wrong.''

"If I was too afraid and you were too embarrassed
by your underwear, what the hell happened? You
want to take a shot at explaining that?''

"I guess we forgot.''

"I guess we did,'' he said dryly.

"I guess we'd better not forget again?'' It was
clearly a question. He knew what his answer was, but
he wasn't certain of hers. The last thing he wanted
was pity.

"I'm driving into town this morning. Want to go?''

She shook her head. "I've got things to do here.''

''Then give me your list, and I'll stop by and pick up anything you need.''

Cleo nodded, stirred another spoonful of sugar into her coffee and shoved it aside. The minute he was gone she intended to call Mrs. Dunn at the real estate office. The sooner she cut her ties here, the sooner she could start the process of healing her heart.

At least this time the wound would be a clean one. With Niles, it had been ragged, ugly, messy.

This time she would simply bleed a lot and hurt like the very devil, and after a decade or so it would be over. She'd forget all about Harrison and maybe even find someone else. A boy needed a father. A woman needed a husband. Someone to love, someone to share her life with. Someone to turn to in the night when the loneliness got too hard to bear.

Yes, and a woman needed another hole in her head.

Fourteen

The line was busy. It stayed busy. Between busy signals at the real estate agency, Cleo opened drawers, cabinets and closets, stared helplessly at the few remaining contents and left them where they were. There was no law that said you had to take every shred of personal property with you when you sold a house.

At least, she hoped there wasn't.

Jimmy was good as gold, but then, he usually was. Sometimes she woke him from a sound sleep to rock him because she needed it, even if he didn't. At the moment, however, she needed to finish packing.

She wrapped a set of mugs that Niles had bought for her from a street fair the first year they were married. A reminder of the best part of her marriage might help her eventually to forget the worst parts.

Her watercolors. Keep them? Glassed work was so hard to pack.

Leave them behind? She would if she thought they would keep Harrison from forgetting her. But then, his preference in art, if he even had a preference, would be something bold and angular, full of sharp edges and hard lines. He was that kind of man. Bold, angular, full of sharp edges and hard lines.

The trouble was, he was so much more than that.

For one thing, he was patient. She thought about their daily walks, with her trudging along like a gravid turtle, when he was so obviously dying to break into a run.

He tried so hard to be helpful. His crooked shelves. The botch he'd made of her yard when he'd insisted on pulling up all her lovely weeds and replacing them with neat little squares of vegetables. A whole package of squash seeds in a single bed two feet square, and those poor, spindly tomato plants.

And all the tools he'd scattered around when he'd tried to change her tire. A tire tool and a jack would have sufficed, but not for the world would she have punctured his masculine pride.

So many things to remember. Their first trip to the supermarket. His gradual "decaffeination," and the resulting headaches he never complained about. The impatience he tried so hard to hide. How could a man be so impatient with himself and so patient with someone else?

Wandering out onto the back deck, a forgotten crib sheet in her hand, Cleo thought of all the ways he had changed since he'd first shown up on her doorstep. All the reasons why she loved him. All the reasons why it would never work.

"Well…shoot," she muttered, flinging herself onto the hammock.

His coffee cup was still on the rail where he'd left it that morning, his newspaper was tossed aside, still opened to the business page. If she tried a little harder, she could probably detect the faintest trace of his aftershave lingering in the hot, still air.

She was still there, still daydreaming, when she

heard the crows squabbling and opened her eyes to
see the man gobbling down the scraps she'd put out
for them.

Armed with a fistful of brochures and a map, Harrison set out early. He'd been dragged to more champagne openings in more posh galleries than he cared
to remember. This time it was voluntary. Before the
day was over he intended to visit every gallery from
Duck to Hatteras. There had to be one that was just
right for her. If not, he'd damned well build her one.

His plan was simple. Inquire about job openings
and study the available art to see how it compared
with hers. He happened to think hers was special, but
he'd be the first to admit he was no expert. While
he'd never questioned his social obligation to support
the arts financially, his interest had been philan-
thropic, not personal.

By the time he'd crossed Oregon Inlet Bridge and
headed south for the next gallery on his list, his plan
had undergone a few revisions. In the first place, there
were no job openings. At least, none in the galleries
he'd visited so far.

In the second place, it was possible that her work
might not be commercially viable. She didn't paint
pretty beaches with waving sea oats. She didn't paint
lighthouses or dilapidated old buildings with rusty
roofs. She didn't paint oversize tropical fish or sea-
shells or wharves lined with fishing boats.

Not that he had any particular bias against those
subjects. Most of what he'd seen so far appeared rea-
sonably competent. The trouble was, none of it ex-

cited him. None of it bore the slightest resemblance to Cleo's simple, understated watercolors.

So he was prejudiced. So be it.

If she wanted to support herself with her painting, he'd buy everything she turned out and consider himself lucky to have it. For all his exposure—the tax value of his corporate collection alone ran well into the millions, and that didn't include his personal collection or the commissions he'd paid his decorator to acquire it—he'd never before realized how personal paintings could be.

Hers were pure Cleo. Deep. Quiet. Deceptively unassuming. He was determined to have them.

He was even more determined to have her.

It was late afternoon by the time he crossed the inlet and headed north again. He'd had one more mission in mind when he'd set out. Nothing concrete, just a vague idea. All he'd needed was a phone book and a few answers to questions such as, Where do I find something or other? Where's the nearest whatchamacallit? Don't tell me I have to drive all the way to Norfolk to locate a whatsit?

His mind teeming with fresh ideas, Harrison was already making mental lists by the time he crossed the Alligator River Bridge. Conclusion: in an area like this, near a national park, with a more or less captive audience, any man with capital, imagination and business savvy—and Harrison modestly confessed to an abundance of all of the above—could write his own ticket.

Cleo knew who he was, because there were still one or two places where the original orange color showed through the filthy tattered remnants of his coveralls. Even so, there was no way she could chase him away or turn him in, not until she'd fed the poor wretch and done something about his eyes. He'd been eating her crow's food, for heaven's sake. No wonder the poor crows were upset.

"More tea?"

"Please, ma'am." He held out his glass, his hand shaking so hard she had to take it from him to pour without spilling. She'd brought him a bar of soap and a towel and made him wash up at the hose outside before she'd let him into the house, but there was a limit to what even soap and water could do.

"You might as well finish up the chicken, there's only one piece left."

He pounced like a duck on a june bug. In just under a minute another bone was added to the pile on his plate.

Leaning against the refrigerator, she studied him. It was hard to be sure, considering the shape he was in, but she didn't think he was more than eighteen. Twenty, at most. He was certainly no hardened criminal. Someone had taken the time to instill a few old-fashioned manners in him, for one thing. "What were you in jail for?"

At first she thought he wasn't going to answer. Not quite meeting her eyes, he muttered, "Got caught driving the wrong car."

He was a car thief. Grand theft auto, as they said on the police shows on TV. At least it wasn't murder.

"Why on earth did you break out? They've been hunting you for weeks. You knew you couldn't get away."

"I had to go to the bathroom."

"Oh, for heaven's sake, if I'm going to help you, I need you to tell me the truth!"

"Ma'am, it's the honest God's truth. We was working on cleaning up that there patch of woods that burned last month, and I had to go, and the man, he said to wait, only I couldn't wait, so when Buck said something real ugly about Ambrose's old lady, Ambrose, he busted him one and Buck, he gut-punched Ambrose, and the guard, he went over to pull 'em apart, and I snuck behind some bushes."

"And?"

"And did it."

"No, I meant, what happened then?"

"Nothing. The guard, he pulled Buck and Ambrose apart and told 'em—well, you don't want to know what he told 'em, ma'am."

She was tempted to call the sheriff's office and tell them to come collect the poor wretch. If it wasn't for the fact that he was all scratched up and his eyes were swollen nearly shut—poison ivy, from the looks of it—she'd have done it, too. But before he'd even got as far as the deck, he'd tripped twice and nearly hanged himself on her clothesline. How could she turn in something so pathetic without first taking time to feed it?

"What did he say to you?"

"He didn't say nothing to me. Casey—that's his name. The guard, I mean. Casey ain't real smart. He ain't mean, not like some I could name, but he ain't too bright, neither."

She took a deep breath and then wished she hadn't.

"So you went back, and Casey didn't fuss at you—so what then? How did you get away?"

"That's just it, ma'am. I never went back. I just stayed there behind the bushes, and after a while I snuck away and just kept on going."

"That's incredible."

He ducked his head. "Yes'm, I reck'n it is."

"What happened next?"

"I run. They was dogs and all, so mostly, I waded. Them dogs can smell on water. Most folks don't know that, but a dog, he'll sniff the air over the water and he can smell where a man's been."

"Then how on earth did you manage to elude them?" Dogs weren't the only ones who could smell. She was going to have to fumigate her kitchen after he left.

"I don't know nothing about 'luding, but I only waded in water that was moving. That way, my smell went downstream and I went upstream and then I come ashore on the other side."

"That was clever."

"Yes'm," the escaped convict said dolefully, "I'm real clever. Ma said I took after my pa that way."

"Well. What is your name, anyway?"

"I was named after my pa, Billy Junior Clayton, but I was called after my uncle Al."

Cleo sorted it out, and then she said, "Well, Al, we're going to have to do something, you know that, don't you?"

"Yes'm, I reck'n I do. You're a-gonna turn me in, ain't ya?"

"It probably doesn't seem like it right now, but it's the best way. You can't go on running for the rest of your life. You need medical help. Once the swelling goes down and you can see again, I expect there's some kind of school program available for a clever man who wants to better himself and start fresh.''

''Yes'm, I reck'n.''

She was running out of patience. Jimmy would be waking up any moment now, and she didn't want the boy, no matter how harmless he seemed at the moment, to know she was here alone with an infant. ''Stop saying, 'Yes'm, I reckon.' If you truly mean it, say, 'Yes, ma'am, you're absolutely right!'''

She waited.

''Well?''

''Yes'm.''

''Yes'm, *what?*''

''Yes'm, what you said.''

The sound of a car door slamming out front cut short her prayer for patience. Her prisoner jumped up from the table and promptly ran smack into an open cabinet door.

''Ma'am, you promised,'' he accused.

''I didn't call the authorities. It's probably a friend of mine. He lives here. He's perfectly harmless, I assure you.''

''Cleo? I'm home!''

''He don't sound harmless.''

There were degrees of harmlessness. Harrison Lawless fit into a category all his own. ''We're in the kitchen,'' she called out, and then had to reassure her uninvited guest all over again when he tried to bolt through the back door.

She plopped him back down in the chair. With his swollen eyes, the poor boy looked more like a tat-

tered, pink-skinned bullfrog than a desperate criminal.
"Now, stay there and try to look calm, even if you're
not. Mr. Lawless is a reasonable man. I promise, he'll
hear you out."

But *reasonable* was another word that didn't begin
to describe the man who burst through the door with
a fistful of brochures. "Cleo, I've got a brilliant—"
He broke off, staring. "What the devil is going on
here?"

Colorful scraps of paper fluttered to the floor as
Harrison moved swiftly across the floor and snatched
one of the utensils from the knife block. Unfortu-
nately, it happened to be a sharpening tool, but he
was too busy glaring at the poor wretch cowering
before him to notice.

"Harrison, this is Al. Al, this is Mr. Lawless. Al
has been—well, he's been, um, camping out in the
woods for a while, but we've decided he'd be better
off going back to his, um—"

"He's the escaped convict. For God's sake, Cleo,
listen to me—"

"No, you listen to me. This poor boy needs help,
and he's already agreed to go back and turn himself
in, haven't you, Al? He's going to get his eyes taken
care of—he has some bites that are infected, too—
and then he's going to get into one of the educational
programs and get his GED, and when he's paid his
debt to society, why, then we'll see if we can help
him get a job."

Harrison closed his eyes and started counting. The
only thing that kept his blood pressure from shooting
through the roof was that "we" business. It was the

first indication that she might have changed her mind about leaving.

He looked from one to the other. From a fiercely protective Cleo to a cowering shred of human debris huddled over a plate full of chicken bones.

"Lady, one of us needs a keeper," he said, slowly lowering his weapon. "At this point, I'm not sure which one it is."

A few hours later, Cleo and Harrison stood on the deck and watched a three-quarter moon emerge from behind a veil of iridescent clouds, turning the shadowy woods behind the lodge into a place of magic. Jimmy had finally gone back to sleep with his little belly full, his bottom dry and a brand-new skill. While she was changing his diaper, he'd managed to get his foot in his mouth.

Poor, pathetic Al had gone back to the correction facility, but not before both Cleo and Harrison had spoken at length to the superintendent.

"He'll be all right, won't he?" Cleo asked now. She'd endured a lecture from Harrison earlier about self-defense and common sense. She'd come back with one of her own about charity and civic responsibility. They'd called it a draw.

"He'll do added time for breaking out."

"He didn't break out, he was already out. He just…stayed out."

"He also drove a getaway car after an armed robbery."

"Well, at least he was law-abiding enough to stop for a traffic light." She'd made it her business to learn the details of Al's criminal career. "I'll bet anything his friends didn't even tell him they'd just held up a convenience store.''

Now that the matter was safely resolved, Harrison was amused at her staunch defense of the young hoodlum. He'd been less than amused when he'd barged into the kitchen, full of plans, eager to enlist her help. His first impulse had been to throw himself between Cleo and danger—which he'd done, but not before making a fool of himself by arming himself with that damned knife sharpener.

If he'd needed something else to bring home to him just how he felt about her, that had done it. He'd have taken on a pride of lions bare-handed before he would ever let anyone harm a single hair on her head.

Not until after it was all over had it occurred to him that he'd just undergone a pretty stressful hour and a half without so much as a single twinge. He took a deep breath and flexed his left arm to be sure.

He felt fine.

Feeling the warm, soft body beside him, he felt better than fine, he felt...

Oh, boy. He wasn't up for a repeat of last night's performance, but he was sure as hell up. Randy as a goat. They stood there side by side, staring out at a sky so bright that not a single star was visible. His arm was around her waist. Her head rested against his shoulder. Whatever awkwardness they'd started out with that morning had been swept away by subsequent events.

Once they'd got rid of their uninvited guest, they'd cleaned and aired the kitchen and then headed for their respective showers. Standing under a needle-spray of cold water, he'd tried his damnedest to concentrate on the clever plan he'd formulated on the way home, wherein he laid out his idea for three separate, but related, small businesses and then tactfully lured her into agreeing to give him her input. While she was distracted, he'd planned to pop the question.

Instead, he'd spent the whole time picturing her under her own shower, wishing she was sharing his. Sharing his bath, sharing his bed, sharing his table—sharing his life.

He cleared his throat. "I did some research while I was out today. Came up with some ideas I'd like to run by you."

"Harrison, I'm leaving behind a lot of stuff. Anything you don't want, feel free to dispose of."

"Sure. Uh, Cleo? As I was saying, I—"

"I'm not sure if there's a Goodwill around here, but there's bound to be something."

"Listen, about what I was saying—oh, hell. Cleo, would you marry me?"

She tipped her face and stared at him, her eyes enormous. "Would I *what?*"

"Marry me? Now, don't answer off the top of your head, take your time and think about it."

"Harrison, you just asked me to marry you. Are you crazy?"

"Would it help my case if I were?" He was tempted to use her compassionate nature against her. "I'll be honest with you—I'm not always as easy-going as you might think."

"You're not? Does that mean you can be bossy? Hardheaded?"

He nodded. "I won't deny I've been called stubborn, persistent, domineering, not to mention a few less flattering terms. On the other hand, I'm extremely, um, solvent. I was named one of the world's twelve most eligible bachelors.''

"Oh, Harrison, I—''

"Wait, hear me out. I told you I'd had problems with my heart. Genetically, I'm probably a lousy risk, but I'm working to improve the odds. Diet, exercise, no stress. You know the drill.''

"No stress. You mean, like this afternoon?''

"Touché.'' His smile was a masterpiece of self-deprecation. "It might help to know I've got a whopping life insurance policy.''

She socked him in the arm. "I don't want to hear this!''

"But you're far too softhearted to walk away when I'm trying my damnedest to propose. At least, I'm hoping you are.'' With the soapy, powdery scent of her infiltrating his senses, he was finding it increasingly hard to concentrate. "Let's see, where was I? I'm better at working with my brain than with my hands. You've probably noticed that I'm not much of a handyman, but you're too polite to mention it.''

She covered his mouth with her fingertips. "Just hush up a minute, will you? It's my turn to talk.''

"You're going to say no, aren't you?''

"No—'' He winced. "I'm not going to say no, at least not right away. First, I want to know why you asked me to marry you.''

"Because—well, hell, after last night, it's no secret how I feel about you.''

"You asked me to marry you just because we had sex?''

"One of us had sex. One of us didn't.''

She felt her face flame. "Harrison, this is practically the twenty-first century. The sexual revolution is ancient history, for goodness' sake! My parents helped usher it in, so even using the most conventional standards, you're under no obligation—"

"I'm not talking obligation, dammit! Look, do we have to discuss what happened last night? It's embarrassing as hell."

"You don't have to be embarrassed, and you certainly don't have to marry me. I know I'm not the kind of woman you usually have—well, whatever it is you have with your women." A sound emerged from his throat, sort of like a rumble. Cleo wasn't sure if he was swearing at her or laughing at her. "Well, anyway, you know what I mean. I'm nothing at all like Marla."

"Marla!" Grabbing her by the shoulders, he turned her to face him.

"I know, I know—you're just friends, but you can't deny you were going to ask her to marry you. Another thing, and this is for your own good. If you backed out last night because you were scared of what might happen, I understand. But, Harrison, I know what the experts say about sex after a coronary. I've been reading all kinds of health publications lately, not only about child rearing but about hypertension and cholesterol. I know the statistics say that married men live longer than—"

"Hold it right there. Do you think that's what this is all about?"

"Well, isn't it? Just tell me the truth. My feelings won't be hurt."

He shook her, and then he crushed her in his arms,

his face buried in her hair. "Hell, no, it's not! All right, I admit that I considered getting married."

"But not to me."

He hesitated. "Maybe not right at first."

She laughed, but it was a muffled, shaky sort of laugh. "What changed your mind? You discovered I'm not quite as flaky as you thought?"

"Don't ask. Not after what you did today." His arms tightened around her.

"I'm not stupid. I knew I could easily outrun him or whack him over the head if I had to. The poor boy could scarcely see."

"So you took in an escaped convict, fed him and set out to plant his feet on the path of righteousness."

"It worked with you, didn't it?"

He rocked her from side to side, trying to ignore a condition that was becoming increasingly apparent. "Do you have any idea what you're doing to me?"

"Driving you up a wall?"

"That's too obvious. What else?"

"Well, speaking of obvious…" She pressed herself against him, shifting her hips for a closer fit. "Sex is probably aerobic, if that helps."

"All depends on the way it's done, I suppose."

She leaned back in his arms, taunting him with an impudent grin. "We could go slow until we found out how you were going to react."

"Slow, huh? Sweetheart, I don't think that's an option."

"What if I did all the work?"

"You'd do that for me?"

Wordlessly, she nodded. God, he loved this woman! If he had a pedestal handy, he'd have put her on it. Come to think of it, the idea presented a few interesting possibilities.

"How long before Jimmy wakes up hungry?"

"Hours, if we're quiet."

"Now, that I can't guarantee," he quipped, chuckling at the memory of last night's shout. He'd never done that before.

But then, he'd never proposed to a woman before, either.

Thank God he hadn't carried out his original plans.

Hours later, sprawled on the hot, rumpled sheets, a warm breeze from the ceiling fan playing over his damp body, Harrison listened to the soft purr of the woman beside him and thought about what had just happened. Happened, in fact, three times.

So this was what love felt like, he marveled. Lighter than air, deeper than space, richer than the assets of all the Fortune 500 with change left over.

Euphoria. That was how she'd described the way she'd been feeling when he'd first met her. Content to drift, to dream—to go with the flow, as her parents would have said.

Not his. They had bucked the flow, considering it a social obligation.

He'd learned a lot from this woman. He had a lot more to learn, and a lifetime to learn it, no matter how things turned out.

"Harry," she murmured. Her hot little hand found his navel. One finger began to explore.

Harry. His father would have gone ballistic if he'd heard his son called Harry. How the devil could his mother have called a squalling infant in wet diapers Harrison?

There might come a time when Jimmy would prefer to be called James. Nothing pretentious about that. James Lawless, he sincerely hoped, but that could wait. At the moment, he had other things on his mind.

"Harry, are you awake?"

"You have to ask?" Parts of him were wide-awake, all but sitting up and begging.

"I was thinking…"

"You were thinking?" he grated, his teeth clenched as her hand strayed farther south.

"I was thinking that if I decide to marry you—"

"If?"

"All right, when," she said, and continued to toy with his personal, his very personal, his *most* personal property.

"When?" he said in an agonized whisper.

"Next month?"

"When?"

"Next week?"

"How about today?"

"Harry, it takes longer than that."

"I can't wait any longer. If you don't stop doing what you're doing, you're going to find out just how impatient I can be."

With a soft chuckle that stroked every ragged nerve ending in his body, she mounted him. Hovering there, she brushed back and forth against him while he stiffened convulsively and waited for the end.

With agonizing slowness she took him in and settled into a gentle rocking motion, her head tipped back, her full breasts swaying. Other than gasps, moans and sharply indrawn breaths, neither of them made another sound.

Later, as daylight began to filter through the white cotton curtains, Harrison felt a tickling, featherlike touch on his face.

He twitched his lips.

"Harry," she murmured drowsily. "Are you awake? You do realize that marriage is about more than sex, don't you?"

"Hmm. Harry. I like the sound of it. New life— new name. What could be more appropriate?"

"Yes, but do you? I mean, I fully intend to try my very best to be a good wife, but I can't promise to change. I tried once. It only made everyone miserable."

"You're serious," he said, amazed. Rolling over onto his side, he propped his head on his fist and studied her features as if he'd never before seen a stubborn, pointed chin, a wide, full mouth—reddened now from his kisses. Eyes that were almost too clear, too expressive. Eyes that looked out on the world with an understanding heart. "Cleo, I love the woman you are now. If a dozen years from now—two dozen years—you turn into someone else, I'll probably love her, too. Living together, we'll both change. For whatever it's worth, you have my heart in your keeping. It's yours now and always. Yours and Jimmy's. And if we're lucky enough to have more children, then it'll just have to stretch."

Seeing the moisture seeping from her lowered lashes, he shook her gently. "Don't clog up on me now, sweetheart. Do we have a deal?"

The slow, gentle way she smiled at him said they had a deal.

Outside, a chorus of bullfrogs tuned up. The wren nesting on the back deck began to scold. From a distance came the muted putt-putt of an outboard motor as a fisherman headed out to tend his crab pots. While in the next room, Jimmy experimented with a few sounds.

Harrison whispered, "My turn. I'll dry him off, bring him in, and he can have breakfast in bed." Life in the slow lane, he mused. Thank God he'd come to his senses in time. If he ever started racing his engine again, mistaking structure for substance, all it would take was one of Cleo's slow, sexy smiles to put things back into perspective.

"You're spoiling me," she murmured sleepily.

"Is it working?"

"Hmm…I guess time will tell."

There was a definite cat-and-canary quality to his smile. "That's what I'm counting on, love."

* * * * *

Here's a preview of next month's

World's Most
Eligible Bachelors

Marcus Brand, a.k.a.
The Guardian
the fierce man of mystery from
THAT MYSTERIOUS TEXAS BRAND
MAN
by
Maggie Shayne

Casey was in her car when she got the call. And at first it scared the hell out of her.

"Casey Jones," she said, answering the phone just as she always did and managing to pass a slow car in the fast lane at the same time.

"You've made me very angry, Ms. Jones. I'd like to know why."

The voice itself was what got to her. And her reaction to it was instant. An unexpected chill, almost delicious it was so intense. That deep, rich tone spoke of secrets. Of forbidden pleasures. Of heat. It made her stomach clench tight, made her lick her lips—even as it frightened her in some foreign, primal way she didn't understand.

And then the words he'd spoken sank in, and Casey shook herself. What was wrong with her? Her home had been broken into, ransacked. Her sister was being followed for reasons she refused to explain, and yet Casey was getting turned on by strange voices over the phone.

She cleared her throat. "Who is this?"

"Do you make so many people angry every day that you can't guess?"

The Guardian. It had to be. It was exactly the way she'd imagined he would sound. Dark, lonely, elusive. Sexy as hell. "Actually, yes," she said. "I tend to make a lot of people angry. But only when I have good reason."

"And what, exactly, was your reason for telling the world that I was in need of a wife?"

She released a long, slow sigh and felt her eyes widen just a bit. "Then it *is* you."

His sigh wasn't wistful as hers had been. It was impatient. "Your reasons, Ms. Jones?"

She ran a stop sign, heard someone blow their horn long and loud and veered sharply just in time to avoid being broadsided. "Damn! Hold on a minute." She pulled the car out of the intersection and onto the shoulder. "That's better. At least I won't get myself killed."

"I wouldn't be so sure of that."

She blinked. "Is that a threat? I thought you were supposed to be the good guy."

"Not to people who invade my privacy, Ms. Jones."

"Oh."

His breath filled her ear as if he were right beside her, and it sent a shiver down her spine. Every time he called her "Ms. Jones" in that deep, sultry voice, she felt heat sizzle through her. And she wanted to hear him say "Casey" in that same mysterious, almost whisper.

"Ms. Jones?" he prompted.

"Casey." She blurted it on impulse and instantly regretted that she had.

She blinked. He was angry. She'd nearly forgotten all about that. "Right," she said. "Look, I'm sorry about the ad thing. I needed to get your attention, and it was the only thing I could think of.''

There was a brief silence. Then, "You...you placed that ad just to provoke me into contacting you?''

His voice softer than before, he said, "I guess it did at that.'' But then it got hard again, even violent. "If you're a reporter—''

"I'm not.'' Casey bit her lip. It was a blatant lie. But it was obvious what this Guardian character thought of the press. If she told him the truth, he'd hang up and she'd never hear from him again. And she needed the guy.

"Then what *are* you after?''

She licked her lips, watched the traffic pass her by but didn't really see it. "I need your help,'' she said, very softly. "My sister is in trouble. Serious trouble.''

SPECIAL EDITION

Stories of love and life, these powerful novels are tales that you can identify with—romances with "something special" added in!

Fall in love with the stories of authors such as **Nora Roberts, Diana Palmer, Ginna Gray** and many more of your special favorites—as well as wonderful new voices!

Special Edition brings you entertainment for the heart!

SILHOUETTE® Desire®

Do you want...

Dangerously handsome heroes

Evocative, everlasting love stories

Sizzling and tantalizing sensuality

Incredibly sexy miniseries like **MAN OF THE MONTH**

Red-hot romance

Enticing entertainment that can't be beat!

You'll find all of this, and much *more* each and every month in **SILHOUETTE DESIRE**. Don't miss these unforgettable love stories by some of romance's hottest authors. Silhouette Desire—where your fantasies will always come true....

DES-GEN

If you've got the time...
We've got the
INTIMATE MOMENTS

Passion. Suspense. Desire. Drama. Enter a world that's larger than life, where men and women overcome life's greatest odds for the ultimate prize: love. Nonstop excitement is closer than you think...in Silhouette Intimate Moments!

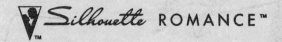

Silhouette ROMANCE™

What's a single dad to do when he needs a wife by next Thursday?

Who's a confirmed bachelor to call when he finds a baby on his doorstep?

How does a plain Jane in love with her gorgeous boss get him to notice her?

From classic love stories to romantic comedies to emotional heart tuggers, **Silhouette Romance** offers six irresistible novels every month by some of your favorite authors! Such as...beloved bestsellers **Diana Palmer, Annette Broadrick, Suzanne Carey, Elizabeth August** and **Marie Ferrarella,** to name just a few—and some sure to become favorites!

Fabulous Fathers...Bundles of Joy...Miniseries... Months of blushing brides and convenient weddings... Holiday celebrations... You'll find all this and much more in **Silhouette Romance**—always emotional, always enjoyable, always about love!

WAYS TO *UNEXPECTEDLY* MEET MR. RIGHT:

♡ Go out with the sexy-sounding stranger your daughter secretly set you up with through a personal ad.

♡ RSVP yes to a wedding invitation—soon it might be your turn to say "I do!"

♡ Receive a marriage proposal by mail— from a man you've never met....

These are just a few of the unexpected ways that written communication leads to love in Silhouette Yours Truly.

Each month, look for two fast-paced, fun and flirtatious Yours Truly novels (with entertaining treats and sneak previews in the back pages) by some of your favorite authors—and some who are sure to become favorites.

YOURS TRULY™:
Love—when you least expect it!

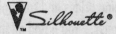

YT-GEN

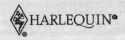 **HARLEQUIN**®

Not The Same Old Story!

 **HARLEQUIN** **PRESENTS**®

Exciting, glamorous romance stories that take readers around the world.

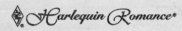 *Harlequin Romance*®

Sparkling, fresh and tender love stories that bring you pure romance.

 **HARLEQUIN**® *Temptation*

Bold and adventurous—Temptation is strong women, bad boys, great sex!

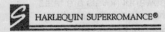 **HARLEQUIN SUPERROMANCE**®

Provocative and realistic stories that celebrate life and love.

 **HARLEQUIN**® **AMERICAN ROMANCE**®

Contemporary fairy tales—where anything is possible and where dreams come true.

 **HARLEQUIN**® **INTRIGUE**®

Heart-stopping, suspenseful adventures that combine the best of romance and mystery.

 **LOVE & LAUGHTER**™

Humorous and romantic stories that capture the lighter side of love.